Ethan Fox

and the Eyes of the Desert Sand

ETHAN FOX
AND THE EYES OF THE DESERT SAND

BY

E. L. SEER

COVER ILLUSTRATED
BY JOHN COLLADO

Ethan Fox Books
an imprint of The Ridge Publishing Group

Ethan Fox and the Eyes of the Desert Sand
Copyright © 2021 by E. L. Seer

To meet the author and learn more about the Ethan Fox Books original series and E. L.
Seer's books, please visit us at https://www.EthanFoxBooks.com. Ethan Fox Books is an
exciting new website from E. L. Seer that can be enjoyed alongside the Ethan Fox Books
series. You can discover behind the scenes information about the author, learn more about
your favorite characters, play games, enter contests, and much more. It is FREE to join and
use and is designed to be safe for people of all ages. Subscribe to our mailing list, join our
Caretaker World Newsletter, join our KidsStagramCLUB, read all about us in The
Residential Daily Star, see updates at Ethan Fox Books KidsStagram blog at
https://www.KidsStagram.com, "like" us on our Facebook.com/EthanFoxBooks page, or
"follow" us on Twitter @EthanFoxBooks.

Cover designed by: John Collado
Editor: Felicity Carter

Library of Congress Control Number: 2021904685

Seer, E. L.
Ethan Fox and the Eyes of the Desert Sand / by E. L. Seer

ISBN 978-1-884573-65-1 (e-book)
ISBN 978-1-884573-66-8 (trade paperback)
ISBN 978-1-884573-67-5 (hardcover)

1. Young Adult Fiction / Action & Adventure. 2. Young Adult Fiction / Fantasy. 3.
Young Adult Fiction / Mysteries & Detective Stories. 4. Young Adult Fiction / Science
Fiction. 5. Young Adult Fiction / Coming of Age. I. Title. II. Series.

Print copies printed in the United States of America

This book is dedicated to my wife, Lori. Without her coaxing and INSPIRATION, it would never have made it past a couple of wacky dreams and an old high school poem. She has been my wife, confidant, and cheerleader – she is my taletaddler.

Thank YOU, SWEETHEART.

ALSO BY E. L. SEER

Ethan Fox and the Eyes of the Desert Sand

Wordly Pagemore's Early Worm Activities & Games:
The Eyes of the Desert Sand Edition

Ethan Fox and the Shadow Princess

Wordly Pagemore's Early Worm Activities & Games:
The Shadow Princess Edition

Ethan Fox and the Kraken's Fury
Coming Soon

Mayhem in the Moongarden
Chapter Book

Received Mom's Choice Award, Moonbeam Children's Book Award,
Story Monsters Award, and Global Book Award.

Contents

The *Ethan Fox Books* Company

Dive into the sands of adventure with "Ethan Fox and the Eyes of the Desert Sand," where every grain tells a story, and every dune hides a secret. As you traverse through Ethan's thrilling escapades, we invite you to extend your journey beyond the pages. For an exclusive peek behind the scenes, visit our official blog at: https://www.KidsStagram.com. Discover the depths of Characters, explore the vastness of Places, unravel the mysteries of Things/Events, and witness the Cutting Floor Scenes that make Ethan's world so vividly cinematic.

Your passion fuels our quest to bring Ethan and Hayley's adventures to the silver screen. If you're captivated by the idea of an Ethan Fox film, join our chorus of voices at our website at: https://www.EthanFoxBooks.com/FanPage, and let's turn this vision into a panoramic reality!

Ethan Fox and the Eyes of the Desert Sand
Journey Map
Santa Cruz Boardwalk
Ethan's mind takes a detour back in time. Specifically, back to Manhattan and the night he attended GothCon with his parents.
The Residence
Back at The Residence, Ethan and Hayley discover many of its whimsical secrets, including: Study, Front Room, Hall of Doorways, Map Room, Grimleaver Attrocities Memorial, Cafeteria, Moongarden and its Secret Wishing Well.
Ethan and Hayley awaken in the Study
The Residence
HIDDEN REALM OF POSEIDON
Poseidon
Tunnel Beach
HIDDEN REALM OF LEMURIA
Lair of the Spider Gecko
Inner Island
Kraken Island
One Two-Tree Island
The Residence
HIDDEN REALM OF SHAMBALA
The Silent Forest
Blind Man's Bluff
The Residence
Back toThe Residence, where Ethan and Hayley visit Market Square and the Gallery of Memories. Soon thereafter, Ethan stumbles upon the mysterious checkerboard plane that houses the Four Portals.
After defeating the Hell Giant, the team returns to The Residence. There, Ethan and Hayley discover Deadwood, and the Deadwood Saloon.
Our journey begins here.
Depicts book travel.

Ethan Fox

and the Eyes of the Desert Sand

INTO THE RABBIT HOLE

Fun in the sun on the Santa Cruz Beach Boardwalk was just what the doctor ordered for the Fox family. It had been on Ethan's wish list ever since seeing it on the Discovery Channel. So, when his adoptive parents, George and Betsy Fox, asked him to choose a vacation destination, it was a no-brainer. It didn't hurt that California was the farthest on that list from their home in Manhattan – and after the events of the previous weeks, that was a good thing . . .

Ethan stood at a railing at the edge of the boardwalk and stared at the horizon while he waited for his dad. The fresh ocean breeze tickled his auburn hair as he squinted at the sun glistening off the waves. The ocean always brought Ethan a peaceful calm. Mesmerized by the waves, his mind raced as he imagined what sort of giant creature might burst up from the murky depths. Sometimes he'd even spot the odd whale or dolphin jumping, but so far today – nothing.

Ethan was of average height for a thirteen year old boy. He had brown eyes, straight reddish brown hair, and a freckled complexion. But unlike most boys his age, Ethan was not obsessed with video games. He preferred to be outdoors.

He turned to scan the crowd, and a young girl caught his eye. He held his hand up to block the bright sun. She stood at a storefront, looking at her reflection in its window. She seemed sad, Ethan thought – like she was lost.

The girl turned and stared at Ethan as if she recognized him. The sun's rays glistening off her yellowish-blonde hair resembled a shimmering golden halo resting on her head. She wore a white sundress with yellow flowers that almost matched the color of her hair.

"Ethan – Ethan Fox!" shouted his father from the snack bar. "Come over here and give me a hand, will ya?"

Ethan turned and started towards his father but then paused to look back at the girl – but she was gone.

As usual, George had bought more junk food than he could carry, and when Ethan got to the snack bar, he could not believe his eyes. George had three jumbo hot dogs, four corn dogs, a large pepperoni pizza, two candied popcorn balls, three bags of cotton candy, and three bucket-sized sodas. Even for George, this was quite the bounty. An octopus would have a hard time carrying all that food.

By the time they carried all that grub to a nearby picnic table, Betsy was back from shopping.

"Wow, honey, you've outdone yourself as usual. How are we possibly going to eat all this junk?" Betsy said.

George smiled and winked at Ethan. "We'll manage."

Ethan's parents had an understanding. At home, Betsy made sure they ate healthy at every meal. While on vacation, she allowed them to loosen their belts, and for George that generally meant overindulgence and an upset stomach.

"I almost forgot," George said as he handed Ethan a handful of coins. "A man should always have a pocket full of change."

After lunch came Ethan's favorite part of the day – the rides. Ethan had done his homework and researched the rides to map out a plan of action. Their first stop was the Haunted Castle, followed by the Pirate Ship, Double Shot, Wipeout, and last but not least, the world-famous Giant Dipper.

Ethan's mom didn't like most rides, but she'd watch her two men have fun on the 'terror rides' as she called them. Betsy loved the carousel and the calm serenity it brought her. For now, her turn could wait until her two men tired out, and that might be soon at the rate they were going. They had hit all but one ride on Ethan's list and a few others for good measure, but they saved the best for last.

"That should challenge our tummies," his father said as he pointed up at the Giant Dipper.

Ethan gazed up at the enormous roller coaster. It got bigger and bigger as they neared.

"Ethan, you can skip this one," Betsy said, mistaking the excitement on his face for terror.

"Are you kidding? Can we ride it twice?"

"You two are going to throw up for sure, and then it's my turn on the carousel."

Two vomit-less rides later, Ethan and his father were ready for a break.

"That was awesome," Ethan said as he stepped off the platform. "When you get to the top – you can see over the ocean for miles."

"Yeah, and that big dip is a doozy. I almost lost my lunch the second time," George said.

"Have you two finally had enough?"

"After you – to the carousel, my dear," George said, motioning for Betsy to lead the way.

A sunflower yellow glow suddenly caught Ethan's eye, so he turned, and there she was again – the girl. She smiled, like she knew him.

"Hey, what are you looking at?" his father said from a distance. "Are you coming?"

"Be right there," he turned to answer. When he turned back, the smile drained from Ethan's face – the girl was gone again.

On the way to the carousel, George insisted that they stop for ice cream, so he and Ethan would have something to munch on while they waited.

"How in the world could you be hungry after that huge lunch?" Betsy asked.

The line for the carousel moved fast. Betsy stepped onto the platform and walked from horse to horse to study each one as if they were talking to her. She finally decided on a white steed with a blue saddle, its head cocked in a majestic pose. She had a bright smile on her face as she climbed into the saddle. Slowly the carousel spun and picked up speed as Betsy disappeared from George and Ethan's view. Ethan waited for his mother to reappear, but to his surprise, the girl appeared instead. She rode a white horse like the one Betsy had picked, and her bluish-green eyes were again staring at him.

They exchanged smiles each time the girl passed within his view. The connection was so evident that even his father took notice in between licks from his ice cream cone.

"Hey Tiger, you've got a live one there," George elbowed Ethan with a gentle jab.

The carousel slowed as the girl disappeared from Ethan's view, stopping in the same position as it had started.

"Go talk to her. I'll wait here for your mother."

Ethan jumped to his feet. He wasn't sure what to say or where he got the nerve, but he was going to walk up to her and start a conversation – there was something about this girl he was drawn to.

Ethan jogged around the carousel and carefully scanned the crowd. Having no luck, he studied the platform and spotted the white horse she had ridden. Disappointed, Ethan realized she was gone yet again.

Tired from a full afternoon of rides, games, and shopping, the Fox's were ready for some leisure time. And, of course, cheeseburgers, as his father insisted. After their third trip to the snack bar, the Fox's headed to the beach for a picnic. They hiked along the coast so his mother could find a patch of sand free of driftwood and sea kelp.

"Perfect," Betsy said as she spread a giant yellow blanket out over the sand.

Ethan's father wasted no time plopping down with his bag full of goodies.

"Cheeseburgers, anyone?" George said as he held up the bag. "I got enough for everybody."

"I'm sure you did," said Betsy as she sat down next to her husband.

Still full from lunch, Betsy and Ethan decided to share a cheeseburger and leave the remaining four for George.

"Your belly's gonna pop if you eat all those," Betsy said.

"No worries, honey, I've got one notch left on my belt. Besides, these are tiny little burgers."

The Fox's spent the next thirty minutes on their private patch of beach and nibbled away on cheeseburgers as they listened to the crashing surf.

"What's next?" George asked as he washed down his fourth cheeseburger with a gulp of soda.

"How about we wet our feet . . . like we used to . . ." suggested Betsy.

"You two go ahead," Ethan replied. "I may go for a walk along the beach if you don't mind." He wasn't in the mood to splash around in the water. He had other things on his mind.

George already had both shoes and one sock off.

"Suit yourself, but you're going to miss out on all the fun . . . I bet you didn't know your mother's a mermaid."

"Just be sure to stay in sight if you go on that walk," his mother said.

George struggled to lift his colossal frame from the blanket. Moments later, he and Betsy skipped off like childhood sweethearts.

"There they go – the *Beauty and the Beast!*" Ethan shouted.

"You're beginning to sound like your father."

Ethan's parents splashed around in the surf like playful sea otters. His thoughts returned to the mysterious girl on the carousel. "Who was she? What was her name?"

"My name is Hayley." A soft voice said from behind him, "You were watching me."

Ethan jumped to his feet and flopped around to regain his balance. He turned to see who spoke to him. It was the girl from the carousel.

"I-I-I wasn't watching you – you were watching me – weren't you?"

"I guess so," she said.

"Why?" Ethan asked as he blushed.

"I don't know . . . I don't remember anything before seeing you. I was just here. I don't remember where I came from or how I got here. I-I was just here . . ." she began to sob.

"Don't cry. I'll get my parents. They'll know what to do."

"At first, I was terrified among all those strangers, but then our eyes met, and it told me everything would be okay. I feel like I know you from somewhere. What is your name?"

"Oh, I'm sorry. My name is Ethan. What did you mean by 'it' told you everything would be okay?"

Hayley fondled the ring on her right hand. It was unlike any ring Ethan had ever seen. Made from a metallic black material and shaped like an infinity sign – ∞ – that bent so her finger could pass through both loops.

"It tells me things."

"It talks to you?"

"I know it sounds crazy. It doesn't talk, but sometimes it comes alive, like a snake slithering through my fingers. Then I just know what it wants me to know – it led me to you."

"That does sound crazy," Ethan said. "But I do feel like we've met before."

"Are those funny people your parents?" she asked, pointing at George and Betsy as they splashed in the waves.

"Yeah – but sometimes it seems like I'm the parent."

They both broke out in laughter. Hayley had an infectious laugh that made Ethan laugh even more.

"Strange – I don't know where I came from or how I got here but being with you makes me feel safe."

Hayley grabbed Ethan by the hand, and a rush of bliss overtook him – like a butterfly was about to fly up from his stomach and out his mouth. He nervously swiped his feet at the sand as they talked.

He drew something with his foot.

"That symbol," Hayley said. "What is it?"

"Nothing really, just a doodle I made up."

Hayley reached down to grab hold of his other hand as she faced him.

"Come on, let's go for a walk on the beach. I need to think things out," she said.

Hayley gently tugged at Ethan's arms, and they started down the beach. He didn't want this day to end. Ethan knew their strong connection was no coincidence.

"So," Hayley said as they strolled down the beach. "I've told you my secret. Tell me something about you — a secret you've never shared before."

Ethan thought for a moment. "I have two, so take your pick."

Ethan could not believe what he was about to tell her, but he felt compelled to do so.

Hayley was rubbing her ring finger. "Start with what that symbol really means."

"Your ring talking to you again?" Ethan said. "Okay, so it's not a doodle I made up. I have these."

Ethan held up his hands. Small white symbols glistened on the palm of each hand as if someone had tattooed him with shiny white ink.

"How did you get those?"

"I don't remember. The story is, my birth parents were in a cult before George and Betsy adopted me. The cult did this to me."

"That is quite bizarre," Hayley said. "What's your other secret?"

Ethan paused. "I have visions that come true," he blurted out. "I realize it sounds crazy."

"That doesn't sound so crazy. I have a ring that talks to me."

Ethan smiled at her attempt to comfort him.

"It's like a video in my head that always starts the same . . . I'm in the middle of the desert, and big blue eyes are peeking out from beneath the sand – they're everywhere. Then I'm somewhere else, watching as things happen."

"And they come true?"

"So far, they've all come true – all but one . . ." Ethan's voice trailed off.

They had walked for quite some time, and George and Betsy were no longer in sight. Ethan stopped.

"We shouldn't go any farther – I promised I would stay in sight."

"We have walked pretty far," she said.

They started back down the beach when Ethan spotted a seashell in the sand.

"A sand dollar," he said as he ran over to pick it up. Ethan handed the seashell to Hayley.

"They're supposed to bring you luck," he said.

"How beautiful," she said.

Hayley dusted the sand off the small disc-shaped shell and exposed a flower-like pattern.

As they continued down the beach, Ethan realized that it was now abandoned. He stopped to scan the area, but nothing appeared familiar, as if they were suddenly on a different beach.

Then, out of the corner of his eye, he spotted a bright blue flash. Ethan turned inland to check it out. A three foot tall blue rabbit with yellow polka dots stood upright at the edge of the beach. It appeared to be an Easter bunny with pastel pink shorts and red suspenders. Ethan rubbed his eyes in disbelief.

Hayley tapped Ethan on the back. "What is it?"

"Don't you see that?" Ethan asked and pointed at the strange creature.

"I don't see anything, but my ring is about to jump off my finger. You're the only one who sees it."

"It appears to be harmless enough. I'm going to take a closer look," Ethan said as he walked towards the creature.

"Wait for me."

As they neared the creature, Ethan could hear it as it waved and laughed like a mischievous child.

"Where is it?"

"Right in front of us."

The bunny stopped waving.

"Happy day Ethan Fox," said the bunny. "Are we having fun yet?" The rabbit sounded like a cartoon character with a nasal voice and giggled as if someone had just told a joke.

"Who are you, and how do you know my name?"

"Jasper I am, but many appreciate Ethan Fox."

"What do you want from us?" Ethan said.

"Jasper wishes to help."

"Do you know what happened to Hayley?"

"And what happened to Ethan Fox. Memories lost and destinies tangled. Jasper wishes to help."

"What do you know about my past?" Ethan asked.

"The answers you seek lie at The Residence."

Jasper scurried off towards an outcropping of rocks. He stopped and turned towards them and said, "The Residence awaits, Ethan Fox." Then Jasper waved and ducked behind the rocks.

"What did it say?" Hayley asked.

"Its name is Jasper," Ethan shouted as he followed in hot pursuit.

"Wait for me!" Hayley followed Ethan.

"He went behind these rocks."

They followed Jasper's trail, and what they found surprised them.

Ethan and Hayley stood at the top of a sandcastle staircase that descended into the dark wet sand.

"Do you see that?" Ethan asked.

"Yes – I wonder where it leads?"

"I don't know, but I'm going to find out. Wait here," Ethan said as he descended into the dark stairwell.

Ethan held out his hands to sense his way and the symbols on his palms began to glow.

Then in an instant, everything went black.

THE RESIDENCE

Ethan's head was fuzzy when he regained consciousness. He heard muffled voices and rustling as he lie on the ground, but now the room was silent. He stood and was now in a sizable study that reminded him of a room in a haunted mansion, except this one appeared clean and lived in.

At one end of the room stood a fireplace with an opening so broad Ethan could walk in standing upright. To the right, a thick golden book sat upon a pedestal. To the left stood a tall candelabrum with four white candles attached to the inside of a vertical circle. The candles pointed towards the circle's center, where a spherical replica of Earth rotated in place, as if held by invisible strings.

Ethan stared at the candles. Each burned a flame of a different color – red, green, blue, and yellow. Yet, unlike an ordinary candle, these defied the laws of physics. Each flame burned towards the tiny Earth replica as if holding it in place.

Ethan tiptoed towards the other side of the room. Tall floor to ceiling bookcases lined the walls to each side, and thousands of books sat on their shelves. On the far side of the room stood two doors, one to each side of a full-length painting that hung at the center of the wall. The portrait depicted an angelic woman hovering midair in a frosty ice wonderland. She wore a flowing white gown bathed in crystals.

"She's beautiful," a voice said, startling Ethan.

"Hayley," he said.

"Where are we?" she asked as she scanned the room in amazement.

"I don't know, but this place is familiar to me."

"Yes," Hayley said, "I've been here before too."

"Why did you follow me?"

"I didn't, somebody pushed me from behind, and then everything just went black."

"Everything just went black," a high-pitched voice mocked from somewhere in the room.

"She's beautiful," a different voice mimicked from another direction.

"Who said that?" Ethan said as he scanned the room.

"Who said that?" said a third voice echoed from yet a different direction.

"This isn't funny!" Hayley cried as she spun around on her feet.

"You do the *Hokey Pokey* and you turn yourself around. That's what it's all about," the voices sang in unison.

"Stop!" Hayley pleaded. "PLEASE, STOP!"

"They don't sound dangerous, more like a bunch of smart alecks," Ethan reassured Hayley.

"Smart alecks?" a voice replied, causing the others to giggle.

"You sound like an idiotic dork," Ethan baited the voice.

"I am not," the voice replied as the other two erupted in laughter.

"Newton is an idiotic dork – Newton is an idiotic dork," two of the voices chanted, teasing the third.

"I AM NOT!" an angry voice shouted back.

A book flew off one of the bookcases and startled both Ethan and Hayley.

"They sound like children," Ethan said.

"Children?" another voice said in a serious tone. "My dear child, your age is a mere tick of existence compared to us."

"That sounded like a grumpy old man," Hayley said.

She had caught on to Ethan's game.

"Linus is a grumpy old man," two of the voices sang out, mocking the third.

"So, we have Newton and Linus but not the name of the third dummy," Ethan said.

"Albert is a dummy – Albert is a dummy," Newton and Linus teased.

"Interesting choice of names," Ethan said. "We're tired of these games – show yourselves."

The room fell silent.

"Albert! Come here this minute!" Hayley ordered.

A red ball the size of an apple appeared on the table in front of them.

"Where did that come from?" Ethan was puzzled.

"Newton, come here now!" Hayley demanded.

A blue ball appeared next to the red one.

"Your turn Linus," she said.

A green ball appeared next to the other two.

Ethan and Hayley stared at the three balls on the table.

"Hey dummies, where did you go?" Hayley taunted, but the room remained silent.

"I have an idea," Ethan said.

A huge grin appeared on his face as he picked up the three colored balls and began juggling. He faintly heard three muffled voices as they laughed and screamed at the same time – like kids on a roller coaster. The voices grew louder as the balls began to grow and unravel.

Shocked by their metamorphosis, Ethan threw the balls into the air and jumped back. A loud popping noise echoed through the room, followed by flashes of colored light that blinded them at first. When their eyes cleared, the balls had transformed into three small creatures, each the color of their respective ball. The creatures were no more than two feet tall with tiny slits for noses and yellow cat-like eyes. They had devilish horns and rows of spikes that flowed down the center of their backs to the end of their forked tails.

Ethan studied the creatures in amazement.

They had long arms with loose skin underneath that attached to their bodies like a flying squirrel. Colorful gold speckled feathers covered all but their smooth-skinned bellies.

"I'm Linus," the green one said as he held his hand out politely.

"I'm Newton," the blue one extended his hand.

"You must be Albert," Ethan said as he shook each of their tiny hands. "My name is Ethan, and this is Hayley."

"You are Ethan Fox?" Linus asked.

"How do you know my name?"

"It's not every day a human shows up at The Residence," Newton said, "especially one named Ethan."

Ethan glanced at Hayley, who appeared distracted by something on the bookshelves.

"Ethan—"

"So, you've met RGB," a deep voice interrupted Hayley from across the room.

Ethan and Hayley spun around.

A tall man entered the room through the door on the left. He wore a long half-black half-white hooded robe and a red glove on one hand. The black side of his robe sported an emblem that resembled the candelabra near the fireplace. Four colored spheres: red, green, blue, and yellow surrounded a fifth – planet Earth. A transparent web-like casing encircled them all like a cocoon.

Unease overcame Ethan, like an invisible hand lightly teasing the back of his neck.

The hooded stranger kept his head down as he strode across the room. He slowly raised his head and lowered his hood with his red gloved hand. He brushed his long hair aside to reveal his face, and Ethan was shocked as he recognized the stranger – it was him!

"Stay back!" Ethan shouted as he jumped in front of Hayley to shield her.

Ethan's mind raced back to the events that began two weeks earlier . . .

ENTER SANDMAN

Silence filled the night air in the Fox household.

"I'm going to bed," Ethan's mom said.

"Goodnight," Ethan and his dad said.

"Hey, how'd you like to check out my new game idea?" said George to Ethan. George Fox was the creator of the successful *Dark Realm* video game series.

"Sure, Dad," he fibbed. Unlike most thirteen year olds, Ethan wasn't much of a gamer. He'd rather be outdoors where the real adventures happen.

"So, here's the idea—" George pulled an oversized sketchbook from his briefcase. "If a tree falls in the forest and nobody's around to listen, is there a sound? Of course." George answered his own question.

"I'm thinking of calling it, *The Ears on the Forest Trees*."

"*The Ears on the Forest Trees*," Ethan repeated.

The words resonated in Ethan's mind as he viewed George's drawings of a lush green forest with small nest-like huts that hung in the trees. Small appendages zig-zagged up the tree trunks – they looked like ears.

"What do you think?"

Ethan paused to gather his thoughts.

"So how are you going to explain a bunch of funny looking trees with ears?" Ethan laughed.

"Well—" George paused, "I don't know yet."

"This one is way strange, Dad," Ethan said.

Later that night, as Ethan lie in bed, his mind struggled to remember something. Like a thought was stuck on the tip of his tongue. Finally, he fell asleep only to wake up the next morning unrested.

Over the next several nights, the pattern persisted, and Ethan would lie in bed, unable to remember something buried in his memory. Yet each morning when he woke up, he felt closer to the answer.

"I've got to get some sleep tonight," Ethan thought on the fifth night as he lay counting sheep.

"What can't I remember?" he wondered as he picked up the notepad and pencil he had left on his nightstand.

He sensed a strange presence and sat up to scan the room. He was ready to confront the intruder and then . . .

Ethan walked in a vast desert as thousands of fist-sized blue eyes peeked from beneath the sand. They were watching him from everywhere, but the eyes did not threaten Ethan. They put him at ease like they were his protectors – Ethan fell asleep.

The next morning, he woke with the notepad and pencil still in his hands. He glanced down at the paper and saw writing on the tablet. Ethan's handwriting was evident, and his symbol appeared at the end.

"I don't remember writing anything," Ethan thought as he read the words:

The Eyes of the Desert Sand

On an old abandoned airstrip in a desert far away, lands an unknown flying saucer in the revealing light of day.

There are no creatures there to see it in this tortured barren land, no plant life there to feel it just The Eyes of the Desert Sand.

As the saucer doors swing open in a misty fog they see, a man from within the saucer from where could he possibly be?

Emerging from the saucer he steps down to the ground, pausing for a moment as he stops to look around.

He carries a flag of colors with shades from black to white, as he plants the flag into the ground it becomes a beautiful sight.

Returning to his saucer as quickly as he came, the doors swing shut behind him like a picture in a frame.

The saucer leaves undetected by the entire world at hand, unknown to all existence but The Eyes of the Desert Sand.

"Is this what I've been trying to remember?" Ethan wondered. "How come I don't remember writing this? I know – I'll show Dad. He always comes up with this kind of stuff."

Ethan headed downstairs to George's study with the notebook in hand.

"Come in," George hollered from within his study.

"Hey, Dad," he said and entered as George tossed a wadded-up piece of paper into a wastepaper basket. "Three pointer," George proclaimed with a grin. "What can I do for you, kiddo?" Ethan took the seat across the desk from his dad.

"You know all those weird ideas you dream up for your video games?"

"Yeah," George chuckled.

"Well – I kind of came up with one, but in a very creepy way," Ethan handed the notepad to his dad. The smile drained from George's face as he read the words.

"Where did you get this?" George asked.

"I wrote that in my sleep. I think your drawings jogged my memories about something from my past before the accident."

"Ethan, we've been through this . . ."

"Eyes of the Desert Sand – Ears on the Forest Trees," Ethan said. "Don't you see the similarities?"

"That's enough, Ethan. There is no mystery. You were in an accident and suffered amnesia before we adopted you."

"What about these?" Ethan said and held out the palms of his hands.

"We've been through that too. Your birth parents were part of a dangerous cult. They marked all of their children that way – end of story."

Ethan left the room disappointed, but convinced that his dad was hiding something.

Later that day, Ethan arrived home early from a friend's house and heard his parents upstairs arguing.

"Always showing him those stupid sketches – I knew you would jog something in his memory!" Betsy yelled.

"You're right, but I just wanted him to live like a normal child."

"I'm home," Ethan called out. He was not in the habit of eavesdropping.

The next few days were quiet around the Fox household. Ethan's parents were on edge, and it had something to do with his past. Whatever they were hiding, Ethan was going to get to the bottom of it.

Ethan was alone in the family room when a gloomy fog overcame his thoughts . . .

His mind raced and, in a flash, he was among the eyes in the desert. Another flash and he was in a dark auditorium with people all around dressed as ghouls, goblins, and other gothic creatures. His focus turned to a creature talking with two tall men dressed in tattered black robes. Chills tingled down Ethan's spine as he realized – they were vampires.

"Ethan," Betsy called from upstairs, "are you ready?"

Ethan's vision abruptly ended.

"Yeah, Mom – ready and waiting."

"Tell your father he needs to get ready."

"Sure, Mom—" Ethan headed to his father's study and found the door slightly ajar. He peeked in and saw George halfway up his bookshelf ladder holding a withered brown book with shiny golden writing on the cover. George pulled three books from the top shelf revealing a cubbyhole where he stashed the book away, replaced the three books, and climbed down the ladder.

"Dad," Ethan said after backing down the hall. "Mom says it's time to get ready."

George plopped into his desk chair and spun around, unaware of what Ethan had witnessed.

"I'll be up in a few minutes."

Tonight, was the third annual *Gothic Comic Book Convention*. Unlike other conventions, *GothCon* was only held at night at dark remote locations and attended by fans wearing all manner of nightmarish costumes.

George's *Dark Realm* video game series had been such a success that it spun off a comic book series, and those too had become successful. As a result, George was obligated to make an appearance for his loyal fans. But this year, George was also the keynote speaker, and that meant tonight was a family affair.

"I'm ready," George announced as he descended the staircase.

Upon seeing George, Ethan's eyes met Betsy's as she quietly giggled.

"You didn't tell us we're going to a costume party," Betsy joked as she eyed George's attire.

"I'm the keynote speaker. I've got a role to play," George said.

Only a die-hard gothie would appreciate George's outfit. A character from the *Dark Realm* series – Rubio, the Evil Minion of Krator.

Rubio's face was a tattered mass of flesh pieced together like a jigsaw puzzle over his exposed skull. He had no nose, only a hole where one should be. His shredded black jacket oozed with blood. Rusty chains wrapped around his waist – holsters for his blood-soaked hatchets. A spike pierced through his right hand while his left held a hook with an impaled rat that squirmed at the end.

"You went all out," Ethan said as they were leaving.

"Fitting attire for a creep-fest," Betsy said.

"Tonight, we ride in style," George boasted, taking Betsy's hand as their limo pulled to the curb.

The limo pulled in front of a dreary hotel. Dimly lit streetlights cast an eerie glow over the red carpet that led to the hotel entrance. Black lights lined the path making the carpet appear black under the darkness of night. They exited the limo, and applause erupted from the gathering crowd.

"He came as Rubio!" someone shouted as the crowd cheered.

"This place sure fits the bill," Ethan said as he glanced up at the two stone gargoyles perched at each corner of the rooftop.

Things were creepier inside. The floor exhibits resembled a giant graveyard, and burning crosses marked the entrance to each. Swarms of bats hovered overhead while headless zombies and other gothic creatures wandered the floor.

"I don't understand—" his mom whispered. "This is creepy. How can they be having so much fun?"

"They are some sick puppies," Ethan whispered back.

He scanned the crowd, and his gaze stopped at a strange creature. A sandman continuously reformed as sand spilled to the floor from its body to merge back into the pile at its feet. The sandman had vaguely defined facial features and two small pits where eyes should be.

"Quite a sandman costume," George said from several feet away.

"It looks so real," Ethan said as he followed his parents.

He glanced back as two tall figures in tattered black robes arrived. They spoke with the sandman and then spun around in unison as the sandman turned and pointed at Ethan. Chills shot up Ethan's spine as he realized they were vampires, and they were looking right at him just like in his vision.

"Time to head backstage so that I can prepare for my speech," George said in the nick of time.

Ethan breathed a deep sigh of relief as he closely followed his parents backstage.

"Ah, ah, all right. I'm with you," he muttered as the words froze in his throat.

After an hour backstage, Ethan finally talked himself down from freakout mode. The moment they had all been waiting for had arrived – George's keynote address.

"LADIES AND GENTLEMEN!" a voice boomed over the intercom. "IT IS MY PLEASURE TO INTRODUCE TO YOU THE CREATOR OF THE DARK REALM! THE ONE, THE ONLY – GEORGE FOX!"

Applause erupted from every corner of the convention hall.

"Break a leg," Betsy said as she smiled and stood on her tippy toes to kiss George.

"Knock'em dead, Dad," Ethan said as George walked towards the stage.

Ethan didn't understand all the fanfare, but as his dad took the podium, he was proud.

"Thank you for the bloody warmth you have shown, and welcome to my nightmare," George shouted to the crowd.

About a half-hour into George's speech, nature called.

"Mom, I'm going to go to the bathroom," Ethan said as he sped down a backstage corridor.

Halfway down the long corridor, he realized that the loud crowd noise had given way to a ghostly silence. Ethan shivered as a tingly chill rushed through his body like tiny ants crawling beneath his skin.

He turned around, and two dark figures descended upon him. The two vampires wrestled him to the ground and forced a bag over his head. Ethan felt a light gliding sensation like he was floating down the hallway. He shuttered at the cold sandpaper texture of their skin against his own. Ethan grabbed one of his attackers' arms and struggled to pry himself free – but he was helpless against their strength.

"Stay calm—" a soothing voice whispered inside his head.

A thunderous jolt abruptly freed him from his kidnappers' grasp as he thudded to the ground. He frantically tore the bag from his head and was face-to-face with not two but three tall figures. Ethan's heart thumped in his chest like a jackhammer as he faced his attackers. The two vampires made a hasty exit through a door at the end of the hall. The third figure stood over him and stared as if ready to attack. Ethan's body went ridged as he braced himself . . .

But a man, not a vampire, stood before Ethan. He wore a long half-black half-white robe and had a bluish-white complexion and long black stringy hair. His long pointy nose stretched from his narrow brows to below his thin upper lip. Ethan trembled as he stared into the stranger's devilish eyes, one green eye, and one bluish-grey with a moon-shaped pupil.

"What do you want with me?" Ethan asked as he and the stranger exchanged stares.

"Everything will be all right, Ethan Fox," the soothing voice said from inside his head.

Ethan could not tell where the voice came from, but he found it comforting.

"Ethan, are you all right?" Betsy's voice called out from the end of the corridor.

He turned towards his mother and screamed at the top of his lungs, "RIGHT HERE, MOM – I NEED HELP!"

But when he turned back to face his attacker, he was alone near the end of the corridor in front of a sign that read:

Men's Restroom

OUT THROUGH THE IN-DOOR

I've seen him before," Ethan said as he glared at the stranger.

"Him who?" Hayley asked.

"The man with the vampires who tried to kidnap me."

"Kidnap you?" Hayley questioned as she stared daggers at the robed stranger.

"I can assure you, Ethan Fox – it was not I who tried to abduct you," the stranger spoke in a low gravelly voice. "We've kept an eye on you, but we are not here to harm you."

"I saw you with the two others."

"Did you get a close look at your attacker?" the stranger asked as he approached Ethan.

"Yes – I saw you as plain as day."

"Then you should be aware of the differences," the stranger said as he bent closer to Ethan.

"Your eyes are brown, but his were creepy, and he didn't wear a red glove."

"My dear brother has joined the Grimleavers," the stranger said. "Mother will have to believe me now."

"Who are you?" Hayley asked. "And why would your brother want to abduct Ethan?"

"We will answer your questions in due time," the stranger said. "I am Daavic Ravenwood. We are well aware of Ethan Fox, but who might you be?"

"My name is Hayley, I think . . . I don't remember anything before seeing Ethan."

Daavic motioned towards the couch near the fireplace.

"Please, have a seat."

Ethan and Hayley sat.

"What are Grimleavers?" Ethan asked.

"The Grimleavers are an army of evil. Creatures devolved and enslaved to serve Victor Qruefeldt and help him fulfill his ultimate goal – world domination."

"Victor Qruefeldt," Hayley repeated. "I recognize that name."

Daavic shot Hayley a questioning glance.

"How do you know Ethan?" Hayley changed the subject.

"How indeed," Daavic turned his attention to Ethan.

"Roughly one human week ago," Daavic explained, "a sandman answered the call of an exhausted human child. He went about his business, sprinkling Z's to help the child sleep. But instead of falling asleep, the child proceeded to write the words to a poem unknown to the human world—"

"The Eyes of the Desert Sand," Ethan said.

"A sandman is a calm and quiet creature. Putting people to sleep is normally an uneventful endeavor. However, when something out of the ordinary occurs, they are very excitable. After witnessing Ethan Fox write the poem, the sandman traveled our world telling the story of the human child who wrote the words of a Creator."

"Sorry I can't help you. I don't remember writing that poem."

"What's the big deal about a poem anyway?" Hayley asked.

"Someone very distinguished wrote this particular poem, and it remains a great mystery. Ethan Fox has become a revered name to many in our world."

"That sounds like what Jasper said."

"Jasper?" Daavic asked.

"A blue rabbit creature we encountered on the beach. Hayley couldn't see Jasper, but I could. We followed him to a creepy staircase into the sand, so I went after him and woke up here."

"Ethan disappeared, so I went in for a closer view, and someone pushed me down the stairs from behind."

"Can you describe Jasper?" Daavic inquired.

"He resembled a child in a blue bunny suit with yellow spots," Ethan said. He held his hand a few feet above the ground, "He was about this tall and said his name was Jasper before he scurried away."

"Jasper, the blue taletaddler—" Daavic whispered to himself. "Is this the first time you've seen Jasper?" he asked.

"Yes," Ethan said.

"Jasper is a taletaddler," Daavic said.

Ethan sat with his hands relaxed comfortably in his lap. Daavic glanced down at his opened palm. An uneasy feeling crept over Ethan, and he quickly closed his hands.

"What is a taletaddler?" Ethan asked.

"Taletaddlers are a child's imaginary friend in the human world. They befriend human children and allow only that child to be aware of their existence. Taletaddlers are the world's greatest storytellers. Many of Earth's famous authors got their stories from taletaddlers."

"You've got to be kidding," Ethan said.

"Not at all," Daavic added. "J. K. Rowling had a particularly gifted taletaddler."

The flames flickered low, so Daavic approached the fireplace and reached into a bowl on the mantle. He plucked out a red marble with orange and yellow swirls and threw it at the base of the brick fireplace. A small inferno erupted and slowly rose from the floor, morphing into a little fire creature.

Ethan and Hayley watched as the foot tall fire creature jumped on a neatly stacked pile of logs and lowered its head to listen to the logs. The creature jumped to its feet and walked to the fireplace where it cradled its log like a mother cuddling her child. A faint whistle spewed from the creature and grew louder and louder. The small fire-being leaped into the fireplace with the log. The whistling stopped with a loud pop, followed by a red puff of smoke. They had landed perfectly into place on the newly burning fire. Then, as if getting into bed, the creature eased itself down on the log and melted into the burning fire.

"What was that?" Ethan asked.

"A firelyte," Hayley said. "The log will transform into a black firelyte diamond after it burns."

Ethan noticed a small pile of shiny black diamonds beneath the burning log.

"How did you know that?" Ethan asked.

"How indeed," Daavic said.

"I'm not sure. I just know."

"They are mine! I saw the humans first!" Albert shouted from across the room.

"No, you didn't – I did!" Newton countered.

"Irrelevant!" Linus rebutted. "I introduced myself first, so I own them."

"RGB – our guests belong to no one," Daavic said.

"What are those creatures, and why do you call them RGB?" Ethan asked.

"Pyrodevlins," Hayley said.

"Indeed," Daavic said. "Those little troublemakers are pyrodevlins. Albert, Linus, and Newton referred to collectively as RGB for obvious reasons, and because they normally find mischief together. There was a fourth that kept them in line – but Kepler's gone missing."

Daavic turned his attention to Hayley. "You, my dear, appear to have knowledge of our world."

Hayley fondled her ring, and Daavic took an interest.

"Interesting piece of jewelry. May I?" Daavic said as he reached out to take Hayley's hand.

"Very interesting indeed—" Daavic whispered to himself.

"I have more questions," Ethan interrupted.

"I've told you enough," Daavic said. "Come, Irvin will show you to your rooms. The Headmistress will answer your questions in the morning."

Daavic motioned towards the doors at the far end of the study.

"Rooms – I can't stay – my parents are probably worried by now."

"I'm sorry, but you cannot leave," Daavic said as he started towards the exit. "You may address your concerns with my mother."

Hayley followed Daavic. She placed her sand dollar on a study table, then turned and winked at Ethan.

When they reached the other side of the room, Ethan instinctively headed for the door Daavic had entered through, but as he reached for the knob, it vanished.

"You can't go out through the in-door," Daavic said as he opened the door on the right.

"The in-door?" Ethan pondered.

They entered the front room of the house.

"Wait. I forgot my seashell in the study," Hayley said.

"Run along and fetch your seashell," Daavic said.

Hayley turned to Ethan. "Come with?" she said as she grabbed Ethan's hand to pulled him along.

They reentered the study through the door on the left.

"How is that possible?" Ethan wondered. He reached for the knob, but again it vanished.

"Ethan, you can't go out the in-door."

"Why did you leave your seashell on the table? What are you up to?"

"I wanted to show you something I spotted before Daavic arrived," Hayley said. "I don't think you got those symbols on your palms from an evil cult." She walked to a bookshelf and pointed to a red book with black lettering. *Secrets of the Dark Realm* by Dakota Drakelan.

"How can this be—" Ethan said. His eyes widened as he stared at his symbol stamped prominently at the top and bottom of the book's spine.

"This place has something to do with my past," he said. "We should come back later and take a closer look."

A commotion broke out across the room as Hayley frantically chased after her seashell while Albert, Linus, and Newton enjoyed a game of keep away.

"They won't give me back my seashell," Hayley said as Newton tossed it to the waiting hands of Albert.

"I've got an idea."

Ethan ran to the fireplace and grabbed a handful of marbles from the bowl on the mantle. He rushed back to the table to Hayley's rescue.

"Catch," Ethan said as he pitched a marble at each of the mischievous pyrodevlins.

Newton held the seashell but panicked and threw it into the air as he reached to catch the marble.

"Got it," Hayley said victoriously.

"Not a firelyte capsule!" RGB screamed in unison. "We hate firelytes!" RGB threw their capsules to the ground, where they erupted into three small infernos that morphed into firelytes.

Ethan and Hayley were shocked as the firelytes each grabbed a leg of a wooden end table, hoisted it up, and whistled in unison as they marched towards the fireplace.

"Let's get out of here," Ethan said.

THE GRUMPLING OF THE HOUSE

Ethan and Hayley returned to the dimly lit front room. It had a massive front door, ample enough for a small giant. A narrow black carpet stretched from the front door to the back of the room, where a tall black slab stood against the wall. A short spider-legged table sat at the center of the narrow carpet, a black leather couch with two end tables stood to its right, and two zebra-skinned chairs to its left. Dark hardwood floors encompassed the room.

"There's no ceiling —" Ethan announced, gazing up into the night's sky.

"It was there earlier," Daavic said, as if it was no big deal that a large portion of the ceiling was missing.

Ethan spotted a baseball-sized soap bubble floating above the spider-legged table.

"What's that?" he asked.

"We have yet to determine its purpose," Daavic said.

"A bubble only has one purpose," Ethan said. "Bubbles are for popping."

He approached the bubble and poked at it, but his finger went right through. He blew at it, but the bubble did not move.

"Must be a ghost bubble," Hayley said.

Ethan approached the staircase and gazed up. The stairs kept going up into infinity.

"Where does this lead?" Hayley asked as she pointed to a door under the staircase.

"That door is strictly off-limits," Daavic warned.

"I wouldn't go into a creepy basement anyway," Hayley said.

Ethan studied the wall opposite the staircase. The study stood to his left and another door to his right. A black chest of drawers stood at the wall's center. A small bench sat to the right of the chest, and to the left stood a giant mirror. Black marble material engraved with cryptic symbols framed the mirror.

"I bet that weighs a ton," Hayley said to Ethan.

Past the study door, a small green box sat atop a pedestal table that stood against the wall. Beyond that stood another door on the adjacent wall, a sign above read:

• THE HALL OF DOORWAYS •

"What is The Hall of Doorways?" Ethan asked.

"A hall with doorways," Daavic said. "I'm going to see what's keeping Irvin." He exited through The Hall of Doorways.

Out of the corner of his eye, Ethan spotted something green streak down the staircase. He turned as a large green moth fluttered through the air and landed on the wall at the base of the stairs.

He moved in for a closer look and spotted a green blob the size of a child's fist. Dark purplish eyes glared back at him and then blended into the wall and vanished.

"Did you see that?" Ethan asked. "A big green— something flew down from upstairs and landed here then disappeared." Ethan said pointing at the empty wall.

"Ethan, look—"

The phantom bubble drifted towards him as if attracted by an unseen force. It came to rest nestled against the wall where the moth had disappeared. The green blob reappeared, popped off the wall, and fluttered over their heads.

"I see it now," Hayley said. She chased the moth-like creature as it fluttered towards the back of the room.

"It wants inside that green box," Hayley said.

The tiny creature landed on the table and tapped three times on the side of the box. The lid swung open, the creature hopped inside, and the top swung shut.

"We have it cornered," Ethan said as he pried at the lid with his fingernails.

"It tapped on the box," Hayley said. She tapped on the side three times, and the lid swung open. "It's empty."

"No, it's blending again—"

"Ethan, the bubble," Hayley said as the bubble drifted towards them.

"Blasted tag-along," a muffled voice said.

The fuzzy green blob reappeared and popped out of the box, transforming in midair. A tiny green creature landed on the table in front of Ethan and Hayley.

"Gruggins McGhee, grumpling of the house, at your service," the creature said as he bowed and offered a handshake.

Gruggins was four inches tall with a mouse-like body and stubby arms and legs. His face was that of a grumpy old man, but tall cartoonish blue eyes softened his grumpy demeanor. A fat bulbous nose like Mr. Magoo's protruded from below his eyes. He had smooth skin on his face and belly, and short fuzzy hair covered the rest of his head and body. Brilliant colors accented his long moth-like wings – bluish-green with a purple and yellow eye pattern centered on each like the eye on a peacock feather.

"That dreaded bubble has followed me around for as long as I can remember," Gruggins said. He flopped back a tuft of his hair. "Every time I cloak, the pesky thing comes right to me. Throws a wrench into the whole cloaking thing."

The hair at the top of his head formed a tall pointy peak that bent forward under its own weight, like the top of soft-serve ice cream. Gold jewelry covered Gruggins from head-to-toe. Bracelets, anklets, and necklaces, as well as a chain that wrapped around his waist several times. Gruggins had bling.

Gruggins gazed up at Hayley, then to Ethan, and then back to Hayley. His cheeks puffed out as a wide grin appeared on his face. He fluttered off the table and onto Hayley's shoulder, where he hugged her neck.

"Miss Hayley finally returns," Gruggins whispered.

"How do you know my name?" Hayley said.

"Don't you worry, my dear," Gruggins said. "Your secret's safe with me – it's got you cloaked for a reason."

"Cloaked?" she asked, "what is that supposed to mean?"

"Not to worry yourself, whatever the reason, it will be revealed." Gruggins said with a calming smile. "Now then, who do we have here?"

Hayley gave Ethan a questioning glance.

"Gruggins, this is Ethan," Hayley said.

"There were rumblings we had unexpected guests," he said as he turned to Ethan.

Gruggins had a slight rasp in his voice. He fittingly sounded like a wise but grumpy old man.

"So, you're Ethan Fox," he said. "Ethan Fox this, Ethan Fox that, you're all I've been hearing about lately."

"I didn't mean to come here," Ethan said. "Please, can you tell me where I am – and how I can get back to my parents?"

"Are all humans this whiny? I'm sorry, but I can't help you."

"You've met our resident grumpling," Daavic said as he entered from The Hall of Doorways. "Are you being courteous to our guests?" he asked Gruggins.

"Always," Gruggins said.

"Irvin will be along shortly," Daavic said to Ethan and Hayley.

"Please Master Daavic, not that mush-mouthed morph-dork. I can't take his showboating theatrics. May I be excused?"

Daavic nodded.

"Thank you, sir," Gruggins said. "I bid you farewell," he bowed to Ethan and Hayley, fluttered to his box, jumped in, and shut the lid.

"Gruggins is easily annoyed," Daavic said, "and Irvin pushes all the right buttons."

"I don't think he likes me," Ethan said.

"Grumplings are leery of strangers, but he will warm up to you — eventually."

"Grumplings were nearly hunted to extinction by the leprechauns," Hayley said.

"Your memories appear to be returning," Daavic said. "Leprechauns fear the grumpling's ability to de-cloak the gold they've hidden. So, they hunt them, luring them with their favorite food — four-leafed clovers. Nearly finished them off until we stepped in and moved the grumplings — all except for Gruggins."

The sound of footsteps echoed from The Hall of Doorways.

"Gruggins McGhee is a goon faced flobbyknocker, and his father wears leprechaun slippers," a goofy voice said as the door burst open.

"Irvin — do not antagonize Gruggins," Daavic scolded.

"So, this is what humans look like — much uglier in person," Irvin said.

"Irvin, they can hear what you are saying."

"If you say so . . . Irvin McGillicutty at your service. Here to wait on you hand and foot as the Headmistress has ordered."

Irvin was nearly six feet tall with pale white skin that resembled candle wax. His smooth face had a vague definition, like a department store dummy. A black tuxedo with a bow tie and a rose corsage molded to his body as if a part of it.

"Irvin will show you a trick, but first, I have chores to tend to."

Irvin reached into his tuxedo and pulled out a tiny pouch. He tugged at a small string until the pouch grew to the size of a trash bag.

"I've been looking all over for this."

Irvin walked across the room and picked up a broom leaning against the wall. He opened up the now ample pouch and dropped the broom in, then tugged at a different string and the pouch shrank back down to pocket-sized.

"Cool—" Ethan said. "Awesome adventuring pack. What is that?"

Irvin looked at Ethan, then at the pouch, then back to Ethan. "A pocket tote," Irvin said with a smile. "And now, the moment you've all been waiting for—"

Irvin leaped into the air and morphed into a large egg with small arms and legs and facial features that resembled Mr. Potato Head. Landing next to Gruggins' green box, he sat perched at the edge of the table and rocked back and forth.

"Humpty Dumpty sat on a wall – Humpty Dumpty was a big fat klutz," Irvin said in a goofy voice as the egg slid off the table. Landing splat on the hardwood floor, the egg cracked open and transformed into a giant fully-cooked egg – sunny side up.

"How do you like your eggs?" Irvin asked as facial features appeared on the yolk.

"Scrambled," Hayley said laughing hysterically.

"However the lady likes," he answered as the egg transformed into scrambled.

"That was awesome. How did he do that?" Ethan asked as the pile of eggs morphed back into Irvin McGillicutty.

"Irvin is a mimic, a member of the shape-shifter family," Daavic said. "But unlike other shape-shifters, a mimic can only morph for a short time."

"Did you know that shnickyrooners and shnackleboxes and things like that," Irvin rambled, "they really only happen to old ice cream cones when giant tree turtles eat dirty diapers in a blue elevator of leaf monkeys making the leftover apple trees take the school bus?"

"Why is he talking like that?" Ethan asked.

"Who knows," Daavic said. "I've learned to ignore his jibber-jabber."

"Any final requests?" Irvin asked. "We've time for one more. Tell me the first thing that pops into your head."

"Tabby Cat," Hayley said.

Irvin morphed into a black cat.

"Tabby Cat," Hayley repeated.

The black cat changed into an oversized orangish striped cat.

"Tabby Cat," Hayley said with a smile.

As soon as the words left Hayley's mouth, a small metallic statuette of a cat appeared at her feet.

"Oh my," Irvin said.

"Where did that come from?" Hayley asked.

"Miss Hayley has summoned a copycat. It must belong to you, and its name is Tabby Cat."

"What is a copycat?" Hayley asked as she bent down to pick it up.

"A totem with exceptional powers. Only the true owner can command a copycat and learn its powers."

"But – I don't remember having one," Hayley said and frowned.

"Give it a try," Irvin prodded. "Spy an object and wish for a copy."

The copycat vanished, and a replica of Gruggins box appeared in Hayley's hand.

"How do I make it come back?" she asked.

"Repeat its name three times," Irvin instructed.

"Tabby Cat, Tabby Cat, Tabby Cat," Hayley said, and the copycat reappeared in her hands.

"Fun time is over. Take our guests to their quarters."

"Yes, Master Daavic. Follow me," Irvin said.

Irvin stopped at Gruggins' table, picked up his box, and shook it vigorously. "The leprechauns are coming, you flying green rat."

"Enough, Irvin," Daavic said.

"Come with me," Irvin said as he motioned towards The Hall of Doorways.

"I'll show you a flobbyknocker, you mush-mouthed, rubber-faced morph-dork!" Gruggins hollered as he erupted from his box. He raised a long tube to his lips, drew in a deep breath, and blew into the end of the blowgun. A dart zipped out the end and found its intended target, hitting Irvin square in the butt.

"AHHHHHHOOOOOOOWWWWW, the grumpy wart-moth shot me!" Irvin screamed and grabbed his butt. "I – I'm changing."

His screams grew louder as Irvin morphed into a purple goose-like creature with a bulldog's face and long clumsy antennas – Irvin was a flobbyknocker.

"Gruggins, what have you done?" Hayley asked.

"Don't worry. He'll change back in a couple of minutes," Gruggins chuckled.

"He does look funny," Ethan laughed as the two balls at the end of Irvin's antennas clanked together.

A few minutes later, Irvin morphed back into himself.

"W-w-where was I? Oh, yes – taking you to your quarters," he said as if nothing had happened.

They entered The Hall of Doorways and turned left. It was broader and taller than any hallway Ethan had ever seen. Huge doors lined both sides of the hallway with no space in between. Where one door ended, another began. Black carpeting covered the floor, and the mirrored ceiling reflected its darkness.

No lights were present, but a gigantic beetle-like creature clung to the ceiling. Bright purplish light radiated from its belly and reacted with the mirror. Light rained down several feet in each direction, abruptly ending in darkness – like an eerie invisible wall painted pitch black.

"Only use the numbered doors," Irvin said. "Except for the ones behind us, they are the negative doors, and they lead to the past."

The light beetle followed as they walked the hallway. Doors emerged from the darkness in front of them only to disappear into the blackness behind.

"Irvin, I need to get back to my parents. Can you take me to that door?"

"I'm sorry, Ethan Fox, it is forbidden. The Headmistress will meet with you in the morning, and then you will understand."

"But I can't stay."

"Here we are," Irvin said. "The sixth door on the left is for Ethan Fox, and the fifth is for Miss Hayley. Irvin has prepared very appropriate quarters for you."

"Thank you, Irvin," Hayley said.

"Loaded your Elemental Modulators myself," Irvin said. "Answer many of your questions the ELMO will."

Ethan entered a room that was exactly like his bedroom at home. Irvin had thought of everything. He spotted the ELMO device on his bedroom dresser.

"That might be of help," Ethan thought. Irvin said it would answer some questions.

The ELMO worked like an iPhone, so Ethan thumbed his way through the screens. Several apps grabbed his attention: The Residence Map, Caretaker Directory, Caretaker Training, and Hayley.

He pulled up The Residence Map and fingered his way down a virtual Hall of Doorways. The thirteenth door on the right caught his attention – the Map Room.

"That might tell me where we are," Ethan thought. "And how to get back to my parents."

"Are you there, Ethan?" Hayley's voice said from his ELMO.

"I'm here."

"Good, my ELMO has an Ethan App, and I guess it works," she said. "Have you sat on your bed yet? Mine is so comfortable."

Ethan approached his bed, and it transformed into a pillowy cloud that hovered a foot off the ground.

"You weren't kidding," he said as he eased himself onto the puffy cloud. "I bet these beds are sandman approved."

"Hayley, I studied The Residence Map, and this place has a Map Room. We might be able to find our way out of here."

"I – I don't want to leave. I feel like I belong here, and I think Gruggins recognized me. But I promise, I will help you find your way back to your parents."

"Good, I can use all the help I can get," Ethan said. "This can't wait till tomorrow. Let's go check out the Map Room now."

THE MAP ROOM

They followed The Hall of Doorways to the thirteenth door on the right, just as the ELMO had shown. They pushed through a giant doorway into an enormous room. Their eyes took several seconds to adjust to the darkness. They were in a vast circular room lit by dim floor lights that ran along the edges of the room.

"A dome room," Ethan said.

The walls curved inwards as they ascended. A thick blanket of fog hung high overhead. Towards the room's center, a small circle of light lit their way. When they neared the light, a black marble staircase came into view and disappeared into the layer of fog above.

As they approached the stairs, Ethan turned his attention towards the floor and froze mid-stride.

"Strike that – a sphere room," he said as he looked past his feet for the missing floor. The walls also curved down, forming a sphere. They were walking in midair at its cross-section.

"Like walking on invisible glass," Hayley said.

"This place is strange," Ethan said.

They ascended the staircase through the fog layer. Atop the stairs, they found themselves at the edge of a circular platform that sat dead center in the spherical room – like a crow's nest. At its center, a woman sat in a captain's chair with her back to them.

"Greetings," she said in a soft voice. "You must be Ethan Fox and Hayley – our mystery girl."

A petite middle-aged woman spun around and stood to greet them. She had sparkling blue eyes and a kind smile that put them at ease. Her smooth rosy cheeks were framed by silky long hair braided into thin strands of silver and black. She wore the same black and white robe as Daavic but a black and white butterfly with four spots colored red, green, blue, and yellow decorated hers. It fluttered around like a cartoon on the surface of the fabric.

"Irvin tells me you summoned a copycat," the woman said as she walked over and stood in front of Hayley. "May I examine it?"

"What's your name?" Hayley asked.

"I'm sorry, where are my manners," the woman said. "I am Jordanna Ravenwood, Headmistress of The Residence."

Hayley reached into her pocket and pulled out the small silvery statuette and handed it to Jordanna. Jordanna turned it upside down and studied its base. She let out a deep sigh and her eyes widened as a tear rolled down her cheek.

"What's wrong?" Hayley asked.

"My daughter's name was Hayley, too," Jordanna said, "and you've summoned her copycat." She held out the copycat to show them initials engraved into its base – H.R.

"Irvin gave this to her ages ago," Jordanna explained. "I thought it a silly toy until I witnessed what she could make it do. Hayley loved her Tabby Cat."

"You can have it back."

"Heaven's no, my Hayley's Tabby Cat chose you for a reason."

"What happened to your daughter?" Ethan asked.

"She went missing," Jordanna said, "exactly one century ago." Another tear rolled down her cheek.

"But it is curious," Jordanna said as she smiled. "You don't resemble or sound like my Hayley, but children don't show up here from the human world every day and summon my daughter's copycat. Especially children accompanied by Ethan Fox . . ."

"Where are we?" Ethan interrupted. "I have to get back to my parents, they'll be worried about me."

"Come sit," Jordanna said. "I'd like to show you something."

"Where do we sit?" Hayley asked.

Jordanna smiled and tapped at her ELMO device as she sat down. Two smaller chairs sprouted up on each side of the captain's chair.

"Come, sit—"

The platform began to disappear as they approached its center, and as Ethan sat, the floor completely vanished.

"—now recline back like this . . ." Jordanna said.

As Ethan and Hayley reclined back, their chairs disappeared too. They were floating in midair at the center of the empty spherical room.

The room walls transformed into a map of Earth – they were hovering inside a gigantic globe.

"This is cool," Ethan said.

Jordanna tapped at her ELMO. The globe rotated and zoomed to the United States. Two green dots appeared, one over New York and the other over California.

"This is what I wanted to show you."

She tapped at her ELMO again. The green dot over Santa Cruz zoomed towards them and transformed into a holographic screen that stopped in front of them. Ethan was comforted by the sight of his parents frolicking in the surf as Ethan had left them.

"We've been gone for hours," Ethan said. "They wouldn't take that long of a swim."

Jordanna turned to Ethan and put her hand on his. "Unlike in the human world, time is fluid here. The Residence allows us to go anywhere past and present. When you two arrived, a negative doorway opened. We can return you to precisely that moment at any time." Jordanna pointed at the screen. "I promise you – I will walk you to The Hall of Doorways myself and send you back. But first, we have other matters to discuss."

A river of calm rushed through Ethan's veins as he sensed Jordanna's sincerity. Then a gloomy fog overcame his thoughts, and in a flash, the eyes were watching him navigate a vast desert. Another moment, and he was alone on a beach walking towards his parents as they emerged from their swim and waved at him.

"Ethan, are you with us?" Jordanna asked as she squeezed his hand.

Ethan's vision stopped, and he snapped out of it.

"I – I understand," Ethan said.

Jordanna gave Ethan a quizzical gaze as she tapped at her ELMO. The Santa Cruz scene disappeared and was replaced by one from New York.

"Let's turn our attention to another matter," she said.

Ethan's bedroom appeared on the screen. A sandman morphed out from a wall behind Ethan and clung to it above his head to sprinkle Z's. Ethan seemed to fall asleep but then picked up the notepad next to his bed and started writing.

"You seem to be in a trance," said Jordanna.

"I don't remember any of that," Ethan said.

"Yet a moment ago, Hayley and I witnessed you appear as if you weren't with us. Like you were in a trance then as well."

"Well, I—" Ethan hesitated.

"You can trust her, Ethan," Hayley said as she rubbed the ring on her finger.

"I have visions."

"Visions – what sort of visions?"

"They always start the same, with me walking alone in the desert. Blue eyes are everywhere, peeking out from the sand watching me. Then I'm somewhere else watching as something happens – they almost always come true."

"The Seers – you've formed a connection," Jordanna said.

"Seers?" Ethan questioned.

"We don't know much about them. Never even knew of their existence until the unearthing of Stravis' journal told us of The Eyes of the Desert Sand, and the Hybrid—"

"Hybrid Child," Hayley said.

"What do you know of the Hybrid Child?" Jordanna asked with concern.

"Nothing that I can remember. It just rings a bell."

"Hybrid Child?" Ethan asked.

"Nothing to concern yourselves with. Just an unfortunate Caretaker scandal that occurred centuries ago."

"What do the Grimleavers want with Ethan?" Hayley asked.

"Good question. Something connects Ethan to our world, and if Victor is aware of what that is, that would explain his obsession with Ethan Fox."

"Obsession—" Ethan gulped.

"Ethan, I must ask something of you," Jordanna said as she gently put her hand on his. "Given what I've learned, I must ask you to stay. You will be safer here, at least until we learn what Victor Qruefeldt is up to."

Ethan pondered Jordanna's request. Returning to his parents might put them in danger. Besides, if he stayed, he might learn more about his past and what they were hiding.

"I'll stay," Ethan said.

"Thank you, and I promise your parents will never be aware you were gone."

The Headmistress stood up, and the floor reappeared as her feet touched the ground. She tapped her ELMO.

"We can discuss more tomorrow. Irvin with show you back to your rooms."

Moments later, Irvin arrived.

"Shnickyrooners and things like that," Irvin ranted as he ascended the stairs. "Did you know that blue lizard faced ice puppets are usually the only reason why light bulbs go out for lunch? And if it wasn't for the singing lips of frozen beetle arms then we never would know how the red trumpet bounces."

"Makes perfect sense, Irvin," Ethan said as he winked at Hayley.

"Shh – don't tell anyone why the little blobs of stinky white sock bubbles are still in the hall pantry next to the elephant poop," he whispered and smiled at Ethan as he had just found his new best friend. "Come – I will show you to your rooms," he snapped out of it.

"Here we are again," Irvin said. "Maybe this time you won't wander off. Trouble you will be in tomorrow – for wandering off."

"We're not in trouble," Hayley said.

"That's what they all say. I sure would like to be a fly on the wall when the Headmistress hands out your punishment," Irvin morphed into a giant fly and landed on Ethan's door. "It'll be curtains for you." The fly transformed into curtains that covered the entrance.

"Give up McGillicutty," Ethan said as he moved the curtains aside.

Upon entering his room, Ethan examined the apps on his ELMO. He found one about Caretaker training that explained their purpose on Earth – they were sent to nurture the human world. Black and white robed Caretakers all possessed the ability to evolve earthly creatures. They used this ability to maintain Earth's ecological balance and ensure that humans evolve naturally. It enabled them to evolve failing species that were important to the food chain, allowing them to survive when they otherwise would not.

Ethan touched the 'Hayley' app and heard her humming.

"Hayley—"

"I was about to call you," she said.

"Hayley, I studied the ELMO app that explains what the Caretakers do. They all have the power to evolve living things, but their laws forbid them from evolving humans . . ."

"Hayley – what were you humming?" Ethan asked.

"I'm not sure. I've had it in my head ever since we met."

"Sounds familiar—"

"What? I didn't hear you."

"Hayley, I haven't told you everything – I have no memory of anything before I was eight years old."

"What happened?"

"My parents' story is that I was in an accident, and until a week ago, I believed them."

"But you don't anymore?"

"No – I showed my dad that poem, and he freaked out. Then I overheard my parents arguing about me – they are hiding something."

"Our pasts, do you think they are connected?" Hayley asked.

"Jasper said something about our tangled pasts," Ethan said.

"I wonder—" Hayley said.

"Wonder what?" Ethan asked.

"I remember things about this place, and I'm sure I've been here before. But what is your connection?"

"Wish I knew," Ethan said.

"Well, I think we should work together to find out," Hayley said.

"I was hoping you would say that. I think we should start in the study. My symbol on that book isn't a coincidence. Maybe we can learn more about Victor Qruefeldt."

"Ethan – I was going to call you . . . I remembered something else about The Residence. There is a room here, a scary room that will tell us all about the Grimleavers."

Ethan pulled up The Residence Map on his ELMO and thumbed his way down the virtual Hall of Doorways.

"This must be it," Ethan said. "The Grimleaver Atrocities Memorial – let's go check it out."

A GRIM REMINDER

Ethan and Hayley met in The Hall of Doorways and made their way to the seventeenth door on the right. They entered a dimly lit room with row upon row of creepy life-sized statues on display. Some of the exhibits were massive and they stretched off into the distance as far as the eye could see.

"House of horrors," Ethan said. "Reminds me of a wax museum."

They approached a golden plaque that read:

**In memory of the brave Caretakers
who have paid the ultimate price in service to
humanity. May they serve to remind us of the
atrocities perpetrated by the Grimleavers.
We will never forget you.**

They crept into the dark room to explore. Light beetles clung to the ceiling and rained light down on each exhibit. Sets of two figures stood in each – a before and after. A gold plaque rested at the base to commemorate the victim.

"You were right about one thing," Ethan said. "This place is scary."

Ethan bent down to read a plaque:

In loving memory of Nicole Knight, survived by her husband, Nicholas . . . she was abducted and devolved into Earth's first vampire – the first of many vampires that now serve in Victor Qruefeldt's Grimleaver army.

The 'before' statuette of Nicole depicted a beautiful woman in a flowing white robe. She had a tan complexion and long ice blue hair that draped down her back between two elegant angel wings. Her facial features were soft and feminine except for the sharp canine teeth that peeked out from her pretty smile.

The 'after' version of Nicole showed a stunning contrast between good and evil. Grim-Nicole donned black hair and bat wings draped in black. Her tan complexion had faded to a dark grayish tone, and she had long, sharp vampire teeth and knife-like fingernails. Glowing red eyes glared back at Ethan as he studied what they had done to Nicole.

"Ethan, take a look at this one."

"This explains why all the doors are so huge," Ethan said as he joined Hayley at another exhibit that displayed a giant about twelve feet tall.

"His name was Gaball. They devolved him into a cyclops."

Gaball appeared to be a gentle giant with one enormous blue eye centered on his forehead. He wore blue jeans, a red plaid shirt, and snow boots. Gaball reminded Ethan of Paul Bunyan.

Grim-Gaball terrified Ethan and was much taller than before-Gaball – at least twenty feet tall. He wore pelts of fur stitched together to cover his body – like a caveman. A long sharp horn protruded from the middle of his head above his now black pupil-less eye.

Ethan peered down the long row of displays, and something caught his eye, another room with a bright light that shined towards them. He started down the row of statues, and a chill ran down his spine.

"Where are you going?" Hayley asked.

Ethan silently continued down the corridor, and as he drew closer, he could see into the room through a broad archway. He approached the backside of a statue well-lit from its front. The chills running down Ethan's spine intensified as he stared at the dark silhouette in front of him.

"What's wrong?" Hayley asked as she walked up behind him.

"It's him," he said. Ethan winced as he glared up at the figure of a tall man. Gargantuan protruding ears swept forward over his head like curved horns.

"Him who?" Hayley asked.

"Hayley, do you remember what I told you about my visions?"

"Yes."

"All but one has come true – and he's in it," Ethan said as he pointed at the figure.

They walked to the front of the statue and were shocked as they read the plaque:

Victor Qruefeldt
Once a respected Caretaker, Victor Qruefeldt is
the founder of the Grimleavers. His murder of
Odin Ravenwood and attack on the Hybrid
Child are mourned in our hearts forever.

Victor later commissioned the Heldrik Vonn
Grim puzzle box and has since committed
countless atrocities by devolving earthly and
elemental creatures into monsters. An army of
evil to help in his crusade to enslave humanity.

To stop them, we have established CAGE, the
Caretaker Anti-Grimleaver Enforcement team.
Victor's crimes against the universe will not go
unpunished.

"Hybrid Child—" Ethan said.

"Sounds like the Hybrid Child and Victor Qruefeldt are somehow connected," Hayley said.

Ethan looked up at the likeness of Victor Qruefeldt. He had piercing red inset eyes and wore a flowing black robe and army boots. Scars covered his disfigured face, and he had no hair. Bony ridges poked up all over his skull and gave his head a brainy appearance. Enormous ears were his most noticeable disfigurement. They protruded up and out and swept forward, coming to points over his head like large, tapered horns.

Ethan began to breathe heavily. "It's like a reoccurring nightmare and starts like they all do – with the eyes in the sand. Then I'm in a room with people around me. I'm not sure who they are, but he walks towards me. A bright light shines through an open door behind him, so only his silhouette is visible – until he gets closer." Ethan hugged his chest and backed away slowly as his teeth clattered.

"Maybe we've seen enough for now," Hayley said as she gently grabbed Ethan's arm to lead him away.

They entered the main gallery and veered right down a different row of exhibits. Someone was standing in the dimly lit corridor ahead. They approached and spotted a woman crying in front of a display. Not your average woman, Ethan realized as he glanced down at her coiled snake-like body.

"Was she family?" Hayley asked in a soft tone.

The woman's body rotated in place as her lower half uncoiled. She had brilliant blue skin accented by black swirls scattered over the length of her body. Her upper body was that of a slim woman's that tapered at the waist into an enormous snake body.

"Sss-she was my sister," the woman said between lashes of her black snake tongue. She had a gentle but hissy voice. A king-sized tear rolled down her scaly cheek and fell to the floor.

"I'm sorry," Hayley said.

"You must be Ethan and Hayley," the woman said. "I'm Brianna." She extended her hand.

"Yes," Ethan said as he shook her leathery hand.

"Nice to meet you," Hayley shook her hand too.

Brianna had pleasant facial features with long green tube-like worms for hair. They were as thick as licorice and moved and shimmered like satin. Tiny faces peeked out the ends and smiled.

"They say the pain sss-subsides with time, but it seems like only yesterday . . ."

Ethan glanced at the plaque and then at the exhibit. The before likeness looked like Brianna but with greener hues of blue. Ethan then turned to the after likeness. They transformed Brianna's sister Medusa into a hideous creature with an enormous serpent's body. Her vibrant colors had drained away to a lifeless grayish-green. Ethan grimaced as he gazed at the nest of black vipers with piercing red eyes that grew from Medusa's head.

"It's-sss why I joined CAGE," Brianna hissed. "We must stop them."

"You belong to CAGE," Ethan said. "Can you tell us about them?"

"We are a small team, at least CAGE leadership is small, but we have hundreds in the field. We've all suffered severely at the hands of the Grimleavers."

"The Grimleavers are very dangerous, so CAGE has an almost impossible task," Hayley said as she rubbed her ring.

"I will introduce you to more of us if you would like. Please join us for breakfast tomorrow, the eighth door on the left."

"We would love to," Hayley said.

BREAKFAST AND A TUSSLE

Ethan awoke bright and early and wasted no time calling Hayley.

"Hayley, you up yet?"

"Yeah, I've been up for a while."

"Let's start in the study today. We can follow up on the book with my symbol."

"I was thinking the same thing. We have time before breakfast."

They headed down The Hall of Doorways towards the study.

"Shnickyrooners and shnackleboxes and things like that. Have you ever seen a chocolate pig play ping pong underneath the fat noodle legs of a purple water rat?"

Irvin emerged from the darkness.

"No Irvin – but I'd love to," Ethan said.

Irvin smiled at Ethan's friendly response. "It's quite like the hair at the tip of a hockey puck's peach whiskers – but not quite as lonely."

"I think I'm beginning to understand him," Ethan whispered to Hayley.

Irvin carried a stack of newspapers in his arms.

"What have you got there?" Hayley asked.

"Hot off the presses, the first print edition of *The Residential Daily Star*. Would you like one?"

Irvin handed them each a copy.

"My very own idea. Caretakers have read the stupid app for centuries, but my new paper edition is the wave of the future."

"Thank you," they said.

"Got to run. I still have these to deliver before breakfast," Irvin said and disappeared into the darkness.

"Hayley, look—"

They studied the paper's front page, a tribute piece called: *In Remembrance of our Fallen Leader*s. A full-color picture of Odin and Ryvias Ravenwood accompanied the text. They were both handsome men and wore black and white Caretaker robes. Odin was slightly taller with long silver hair that fell below his shoulders. Ryvias resembled his dad Odin, but had long black hair and a darker complexion.

Ethan and Hayley read the article below the pictures. There weren't many details, but it did say that Odin Ravenwood was the second Caretaker headmaster. His friend, Victor Qruefeldt, stabbed him in the back so Victor could harvest the rib of the infant Hybrid Child.

"Why would Victor want an infant's rib?" Hayley asked.

"I don't know, but the story of the Hybrid Child keeps popping up everywhere."

The study sat empty when they arrived, so they beelined for the book with Ethan's symbol. He pulled it from the shelf and read the title out loud.

"*Secrets of the Dark Realm* by Dakota Drakelan. The Dark Realm—" he repeated. "My dad's video game has a Dark Realm. I always thought he made it up."

Ethan turned to a page that described Dakota Drakelan.

"It says here that Dakota Drakelan is an expert on dark forces, the black arts, and creational sciences. He is a controversial Caretaker figure due to his belief in the existence of a hidden Dark Realm."

Ethan thumbed through more pages and stopped at one with pictures.

"These creatures are in my dad's game, he has connections to this place, and this is proof."

"Maybe we should talk to this Dakota Drakelan," Hayley said.

"Great idea."

Hayley spotted a title that caught her eye. *Weapons and Other Dangerous Inventions of the Chrysalis.*

She flipped through several pages and stopped on one that gripped her attention.

"Ethan, check this out," she showed him a picture of a small black metallic box. Hayley's infinity ring lay nestled inside. The paragraph next to the photo explained that the ring was a rift-key, crafted from the Hybrid Child's rib to power the Heldrik Vonn Grim puzzle box. Heldrik created only one – for Victor Qruefeldt. It was the most feared weapon in existence with known capabilities: soul reaping, rift jumping, teleportation, and instant death.

"Hybrid Child—" Ethan said. "Victor needed the child's rib for the rift-key."

"I wonder how it ended up on my finger? He must realize it's missing."

"He must, and we need to make sure he doesn't get it back."

Ethan and Hayley's findings disturbed them. They stayed in the study for another hour until Ethan's stomach growled.

"Sounds like somebody is hungry," Hayley said. "Brianna said they serve breakfast in room 8L."

"Yeah, let's go so that I can quiet my belly."

They entered a huge dining hall with white floors and a kitchen. The kitchen was a fully equipped chef's station, and in the dining area, tables were full of patrons that wore black and white Caretaker robes. An antique piano and bench stood against the wall. In the corner was a gigantic chair with legs that were nearly as tall as Ethan.

"Chef Irvin is slaving away," Irvin said from the kitchen as the top of his head morphed into a tall chef's hat.

"I'm pleased you came to join us," Brianna called out from a table. She sat coiled in a chair next to Daavic and another Caretaker as she waved them over.

Brianna and her tablemates politely rose to greet them.

"You've met Daavic," she said.

Daavic smiled and waved his red gloved hand.

"This is Nicholas Knight," Brianna gestured towards a tall man that stood to Ethan's left.

Nicholas had a muscular build and a tanned complexion, and piercing black pupils accented his pale blue eyes. He wore a long white robe with gold trim, and long white hair fell well past his shoulders. Behind his back, bulky angel wings protruded outside his robe.

"Hi—" Ethan stopped in mid-sentence, startled by the sharp canines that peeked out as Nicholas smiled.

"A pleasure to meet you," Hayley said with a smile.

"Unfortunately, Alexander Sturgis is on a secret mission, but Azron should be along sss-shortly."

"Alexander is always getting called away," Nicholas said. "Ever since he took over for old Dakota."

Ethan and Hayley looked at each other and then took their seats.

"Who is Dakota?" Ethan asked.

"A tired, crazy old man—" Daavic answered.

"He was our master of dark studies."

"He is Alexander's mentor," Nicholas said.

"Enough about that old coot," Daavic said.

"Are you all CAGE members?" Hayley asked.

"We are, and I for one am grateful," said Nicholas.

"As am I – to serve a noble purpose at such a terrible time has been lifesaving," Brianna said.

Nicholas nodded. "When I lost my Nicole, I thought life no longer had meaning."

"We viewed her statue in the Memorial," Hayley said. "She was beautiful, and what they did to her was horrible."

Ethan stared at Nicholas's teeth as a broad smile appeared around his pointy canines.

"Do I frighten you?" he asked Ethan. "Vamprils have no taste for blood – I can assure you."

"Vamprils once served as Caretakers in great numbers," Brianna said, "but after Nicole's abduction – only Nicholas remains."

The silverware on the table started to vibrate as the floor lightly trembled. A sizable shadow appeared as a small giant approached. He carried the huge chair to their table and sat. Even after sitting, he towered over the rest of their group. A section of the table rose to accommodate his height.

"Azron, these are our visitors – Ethan and Hayley, meet Azron," Brianna said.

Azron's enormous size took up nearly half of the table. He had scraggly black hair and thick whiskers that resembled burnt rice. Ethan gazed into the single oversized eye that bulged from Azron's forehead. He did not speak but greeted Ethan and Hayley with a friendly smile and gently offered his hand.

"Are you a CAGE member too, Azron?" Ethan asked as he shook Azron's pinky finger. But Azron did not speak and only smiled.

"You'll have to excuse Azron," Nicholas said. "Giants are shy around strangers, but he will warm up to you."

Irvin approached their table.

"If I may interrupt, Master Daavic. May I take your orders?"

"Certainly."

"I assume most of you will have the usual," Irvin said. "Brianna – one gopher ham and rat cheese omelet. Nicholas – one blood turnip, a side of buttermilk toad muffins, and a glass of dragon's milk. Master Daavic – two double-yolked eggs suns-up, waffled fish stick hash browns, and a dash of pickle dust. Azron – three platters of pancake leaves drizzled with melted peacock butter. Moonflowers sent a fresh pancake shrub just this morning."

Irvin turned to Ethan and Hayley.

"Our menu probably sounds strange," Brianna said.

Ethan's confusion must have been apparent.

"Our evolutioneer abilities allow us to grow plant-based foods into any concoction you might imagine – four-legged chickens, chocolate frogs – you name it."

"Our Mrs. Moongarden is quite the magician when it comes to growing things," Nicholas said. "Green fingers I believe the humans call it."

"Green thumb," Ethan corrected with a laugh.

The table broke out in laughter.

"Rest assured that no blood was spilled for your breakfast," Daavic added.

"What would our guests like?" Irvin asked.

"I'd like—" Hayley paused to think of something strange, "—an egg with three heart-shaped yolks, on a piece of apple toast, and a glass of blue peppermint milk."

"The number five," Irvin said as he smiled and jotted down Hayley's order. "And Ethan Fox?"

"I'll have . . . a piece of green chocolate toast, with two caramel yoked eggs on a bed of butterscotch leaves."

"Coming right up."

"Can I help?" Ethan asked as he stood and followed Irvin to the kitchen.

"Chef Irvin needs no assistance. I conjure flavors that make chef Ramsey jealous."

It amazed Ethan as he witnessed Irvin stir, shake, flip, sprinkle, and sort. Arms morphed from his body as Irvin showed off. He cooked every dish at once and needed no help doing so – Irvin McGillicutty had mad cooking skills.

A bowl of colorful cereal grabbed Ethan's attention. They looked like Fruit Loops, so Ethan slyly reached over and snuck a few. He turned away from Irvin as he popped them into his mouth. Delight quickly turned to disgust as these loops didn't taste like the sugary sweet flavor Ethan expected. These tasted like rotten fish and were slimy inside, so he spat them out.

"Ethan Fox ate grumpling food – Ethan Fox ate grumpling food," Irvin chanted as he handed Ethan a glass of water.

Their table erupted with laughter as Ethan gulped down the water.

"I thought grumplings ate four-leaf clovers," Ethan said.

"Four-leaf clovers are their favorite food," Daavic said, "but they like Rainbow Hoops too, especially Fish Gut and Snail."

Again, the table roared with laughter. Moments later – Irvin served breakfast.

"I can't believe this," Hayley said as her breakfast arrived. "Three heart-shaped yolks."

"Sure beats grumpling food," Ethan said.

The table erupted in laughter once again.

A four-armed woman with a red beehive hairdo interrupted their breakfast.

"Master Daavic," she said, "I am compelled to remind you of this morning's CAGE meeting – I am secretary after all, and attendance is most essential."

"Yes, Bella – we were just about to leave," Daavic said.

Bella had a yappy singsong voice that reminded Ethan of the nosey next-door neighbor type.

"I couldn't help but notice your breakfast companions. I've so looked forward to meeting our guests," she said.

"Bella Wentworth – Ethan Fox and Hayley," Daavic said.

"Pleased to meet you," Bella said. "I would love to sit down and chat – but duty calls, I must run along and prepare for the meeting."

Bella headed for the door but then stopped and turned back.

"I nearly forgot Master Daavic. My Boris has been missing for weeks now, so I think it's time for me to join CAGE in an official capacity."

"Bella, there is no evidence that Grimleavers even abducted your husband – but we can discuss this later." Daavic waved his hand and dismissed Bella.

"He's probably hiding in a closet somewhere," Daavic whispered.

The other CAGE members chuckled.

"We do have a meeting to attend," Daavic said.

"We wouldn't want to keep Bella waiting," Nicholas said. "She'll appoint herself CAGE leader faster than you can blink."

The breakfast room emptied by the time the CAGE members adjourned. Ethan and Hayley were finishing their meals when the piano in the dining area began to play. The piano appeared to be playing itself, but a small translucent figure was barely visible on the bench. Ethan's gaze met Hayley's as they realized the song was the one Hayley had been humming the night before.

"Who's playing that?" Hayley asked in a loud voice. She jumped out of her chair and approached the piano.

"How do you know that song?"

The music stopped as the creature bolted out the door to The Hall of Doorways.

Hayley pursed her lips. "Why did he run away?"

"Pepper is easily frightened, ever since his abduction," Irvin said. "Even taletaddlers are not immune to the evils of Victor Qruefeldt."

"Pepper is a taletaddler?" Ethan asked.

"Was a taletaddler."

"Where did he go?" Hayley asked.

"He normally runs to Gruggins when he is upset."

"I'm going after him," Hayley said.

Ethan and Hayley headed down The Hall of Doorways and heard a commotion as they approached the door to the front room.

"They're going to eat Pepper alive," the chants sounded as they entered.

It was quickly apparent that RGB were up to no good, but this time they had help. A teenage boy and girl with a ferocious four-legged pet were encouraging RGB to frighten Pepper.

"A burning fire-jay!" Albert shouted.

His forked tail rose, a red fireball formed between the forks, then shot out the end and transformed into a flaming red bird. The fire-jay zipped around the room and swooped at Pepper as a menacing screech erupted from the apparition.

"And a swarm of horned blue-goats!" Newton hollered as a blue fireball shot from his tail and exploded into a swarm of tiny blue-winged goats.

Linus shot a green fireball from his tail. "And a greenie meanie!"

The greenie meanie turned into a flaming green head that resembled something out of a *Ghostbusters* movie, but this one wore a menacing scowl and floated around directing obscenities at Pepper.

"STOP THIS NOW!" Hayley shouted.

Startled, RGB and the teenaged troublemakers turned to face their confronters as the flaming apparitions vanished in a puff of smoke.

The teen boy and girl approached Ethan and Hayley with their vicious pet.

"Look, Caden, our uninvited trespassers have come to join us," the girl said.

"We don't like trespassers. I should sic Malik on them," the boy said.

The teen's pet creature stepped forward, bared its sharp teeth, and growled at Ethan and Hayley.

Ethan looked into the creature's eyes. He held out his hands towards the beast, and the symbols on his palms began to glow. The creature stopped growling and walked to Ethan's feet, where it sat and let out a submissive cry. Ethan bent down and petted the animal.

"What kind of freak are you?" Caden said. "What have you done to Malik?"

"WHAT'S GOING ON HERE?" Gruggins erupted from his box. "Who is disturbing my nap?"

Gruggins directed his anger at RGB.

"Teasing Pepper again – I warned you, didn't I? If you ever did this again, I would think up a dreadful punishment!"

"Yes – Master Gruggins, we are very sorry," Linus said.

Newton and Albert nodded in agreement.

"If this happens again," Hayley said, "you will all spend the night locked in a box of firelyte capsules."

"No – not firelyte capsules," RGB cried out. They joined hands and bolted up the staircase. "Please, please, please . . ."

Their voices grew faint as they disappeared up the stairs.

"Well done," Gruggins said and smiled at Hayley. Then he turned his attention to the teen instigators.

"Blair Trabblemore, trouble follows you everywhere. Take your pet monster and leave immediately."

Blair Trabblemore wore a tapestry of red and black fabric wrapped around her slim body, arms, and legs like interwoven serpents. Her hair matched her wardrobe, crimson red strands braided with black. She had a pointed nose and chin, with eyebrows that curved upwards over her dark brown eyes. She was attractive, but wore a permanently wicked scowl – Blair Trabblemore was the original mean girl.

"We were leaving anyway – Grumpling," Blair said. "Can't stand the stench of humans."

Blair's boyfriend's name was Caden Stanley, a tall boy that towered over Ethan. He had blond hair, blue eyes, and high cheekbones. Caden was handsome with a sadistic streak – the perfect match for Blair.

Caden's pet Malik was a brutehound – a thick muscular dog-like reptilian with stubby legs. He resembled a prehistoric bulldog with razor-sharp teeth.

"Step aside—" Caden bumped Ethan on their way to The Hall of Doorways.

"You'll be sorry for that," Hayley said.

Blair faced Hayley. "What are you going to do about it?"

"Enough!" Gruggins ordered.

Blair, Caden, and Malik exited the room.

"How did you do that?" Hayley asked Ethan. "How did you calm that brutehound so easily?"

"I'm not sure. But – I could sense what that animal was feeling, and could speak to him."

"You were amazing," Hayley said.

"Who were those charming people?" Ethan asked.

"Blair Trabblemore, seems like I've disliked her forever," Hayley said and rubbed her ring finger.

"The Trabblemores are all mean," Gruggins said. "They blame your family for everything."

"Who's family?" Ethan asked.

Gruggins glanced at Hayley, then back at Ethan.

"Never you mind – nosy," Gruggins said.

A whimpering sound broke the tension.

"We still have work to do," Gruggins said.

They could barely make out the shape of Pepper cowering beneath the bench.

"Nobody is going to hurt you," Hayley said. "I'm sorry I frightened you. The song you played – I've heard it before," she said and then hummed the tune, "hmm-hmm hmm hmm-hmm . . ."

"It's working," Gruggins said.

Pepper emerged from beneath the bench and rose to his feet.

"Pepper, this is Hayley, and this is Ethan Fox," Gruggins said.

Closer up, Pepper wasn't as transparent. Tiny black specks swirled around his body – like flakes of pepper floating inside a body of clear gelatin.

"You're welcome," Ethan said to Pepper.

"You can hear him?" Gruggins asked Ethan.

"He thanked us for coming to his rescue," Ethan said.

"Evidently, Ethan Fox can speak with all manner of creatures," Gruggins said.

"Pepper can't speak?" Hayley asked.

"Not exactly. He communicates by manipulating the crystals within his body."

The specks arranged themselves into words on Pepper's chest.

"Greetings," Pepper said.

Then a sentence took its place, "Happy to meet Ethan Fox and Hayley." Pepper extended his hand as the black specks arranged themselves into facial features – Pepper smiled.

Ethan gently shook Pepper's hand, it felt like firm Jell-O and looked like that of a giant gummy bear.

"I'm happy to meet you," Ethan said.

"Ethan Fox might have some redeeming qualities after all," Gruggins said to Hayley.

Ethan noticed something in the front room had changed. The giant mirror had moved to a different wall, to the left of The Hall of Doorways.

"Wasn't that mirror over there before?" Ethan asked.

"Yes – and it's been here – and over there – and there," Gruggins said as he pointed around the room.

Ethan appeared puzzled.

"We have never moved it, yet it always finds someplace new."

"Well, my dear," Gruggins said to Hayley. "Off I go to my secret napping hole where nobody can find me."

Gruggins fluttered towards The Hall of Doorways. The door mysteriously opened, and he was gone.

"He doesn't like me," Ethan said.

"Gruggins has a kind heart," Pepper spelled out. "He's been a good friend."

Daavic entered through The Hall of Doorways and didn't realize Ethan and Hayley were in the front room. He proceeded to the basement door, pulled a skeleton key from his robe, and shoved it into the lock. Daavic paused and spotted Ethan, Hayley, and Pepper watching him.

"Run along," Daavic said as he opened the door and disappeared into the basement.

Hayley was rubbing her ring finger, but this time Ethan felt it too – Daavic was up to something.

Ethan and Hayley said goodbye to their new friend, and as they walked The Hall of Doorways, Ethan was pleasantly surprised when Hayley held his hand.

"You rubbed your hand," Ethan said. "Your ring told you something about Daavic, didn't it?"

"Nothing certain, just a feeling. I'm more interested in what Gruggins said to me. He said – the Trabblemores blame your family for everything. I think he was talking about my family, and he knows who I am."

As they approached their rooms, a rattling sound echoed from the darkness. The light from their light beetle merged with one above Bella Wentworth as she tapped on Ethan's door in rapid succession with each of her four hands. She was quite happy to see them.

"I've come to welcome you," Bella said. "Your arrival has rattled our CAGE," she continued, laughing at her own joke. "Caught our Headmistress off-guard, I'm afraid. Poor dear has been through so much."

Ethan realized that Bella loved to gossip and could be a treasure trove of information. He opened the door to his room and gave Hayley a wink.

"I'm glad you dropped by," he said and smiled. "What do you mean, she has been through so much?"

"Not for me to say, really – but the Ravenwoods have not fared well as headmasters. Jordanna is our first Headmistress after she took over for her dead husband, who took over for his dead father. Can you imagine losing a husband, daughter, and son all at the same time . . ."

"What happened?" Hayley asked.

"Damien Ravenwood killed his father – Headmaster Ryvias – and later abducted his sister Hayley."

"What happened to the daughter?" Hayley asked.

"She was never seen again. Damien is widely believed to have killed his sister too – but Jordanna, the poor dear, refuses to believe that."

Bella waved her four-arms around in dizzying hand gestures as she spoke.

"Damien is Daavic's brother?" Ethan asked.

"Yes," Bella replied. "Daavic witnessed the whole thing."

"Were Damien and Daavic close?" Ethan asked.

"Inseparable, they played in the Moongarden all hours of the day – used to drive Mildred crazy. When they grew older, something came between them."

"Mildred—" Hayley repeated.

"Mildred Moongarden," Bella said. "Old Moonshoes is a close friend of the Headmistress. She could tell you stories about those boys."

Bella blabbered off topic like a runaway freight train, and Ethan had heard enough, so he made up an excuse and told Bella they were late meeting Irvin to help with his chores.

After Bella's departure, Ethan and Hayley were left with a new avenue to explore.

"Mildred Moongarden," Hayley said. "Maybe we can learn more about Daavic and his brother from her."

"Can't hurt," Ethan said.

THE MOONGARDEN

Ethan and Hayley agreed to visit the Moongarden and then track down Dakota Drakelan later. They quickly found the Moongarden with the help of his ELMO – the twenty-first and twenty-second doors on the right.

They found themselves outdoors under a blue sky and scattered clouds. The Moongarden resembled a tropical garden with dirt walkways and picket fences that divided the numerous plant species.

"I've never seen such colors," Ethan said.

"Pleased you appreciate my labors – simply tickled," a voice said from behind a row of shrubs. "Tending to troubled butterfly shrubs has certainly put a bee in my bonnet."

Ethan's eyes scanned the lively shrubbery. Brilliantly colored flowers clung to the stems like butterflies; their wings opened and closed as if ready to take flight.

"Mildred Moongarden at your service," a woman said as she emerged from the shrubs.

Mrs. Moongarden was a short, plump woman with gray hair. She wore a flowered bonnet and had rosy cheeks and a kind smile. Circular glasses perched on her round face – she looked like someone's grandmother.

"My name is Hayley, and this is Ethan."

"More fun than a basket of daisies," Mrs. Moongarden said. "You must be very relevant – a negative doorway appeared after you, they tell me."

Ethan and Hayley looked at one another and then back at Mrs. Moongarden.

"You were adoring my Lisa," she said to Ethan.

"Lisa?"

"The butterfly shrub – silly. She told you her name, weren't you listening?"

"Mrs. Moongarden," Hayley said. "We spoke with Bella, and she said—"

"Bella Wentworth, a bantering Betty that one is, I bet she talked both your ears off."

"She did talk a lot," Hayley said. "She said Daavic and his brother used to play here."

Mrs. Moongarden's face lit up. "Oh yes, I haven't been reminded of the twins in quite some time."

"Could you tell us about them?" Ethan asked.

"I've rounds to attend, but you are welcome to tag along. I'll show you the boys' favorites."

A serious expression crept over Mrs. Moongarden's face.

"I must warn you though, do not wander off. Stick with old Moonshoes, and you'll be safe," she said and started down a dirt walkway.

Ethan and Hayley followed.

"That giant red flower must be the size of a car," Ethan said.

"Wendy is a withering froo," Mrs. Moongarden said. "Do you see the clusters of berries? Froo-berries are a delicacy, but very hard to come by."

As they approached the giant flower, Mrs. Moongarden smiled.

In the blink of an eye, the giant leaves beneath the flower snapped shut, encasing it in a balled up wad. The color drained from the green ball of leaves as they turned a grayish brown – like a giant wad of tree bark.

"And that is why she is called a withering froo," Mrs. Moongarden chuckled. "The boys would try to sneak up on Wendy and steal her berries. Damien was convinced they could, but Daavic grew tired of the challenge—darkness got into that one."

"Don't you mean Damien?" Ethan asked. "I thought Damien killed his father."

"Bigmouth Bella strikes again," Mrs. Moongarden replied. "Damien would never—"

"What's that odor?" Hayley asked.

"Smells like rain," Ethan said.

"Ozone – how delightful – we are in for a dilly of a treat."

Mrs. Moongarden hurried down the path, and they followed. She stopped at a group of small trees surrounded by a white picket fence.

"The scent of ozone always precedes the dance of the trembling nomads."

"Why are they fenced in?" Ethan asked.

"See for yourself," Mrs. Moongarden replied.

The trembling nomads resembled small penguin-shaped evergreens. They were three to four feet tall with small arm-like branches that hung at their sides. At their base, they each had two trunks that resembled legs.

"They look like little people," Hayley said.

"Why were they planted so randomly?" Ethan asked. "If you lined them up, they'd look like little soldiers."

Suddenly, the tiny trees trembled violently as if shivering. Then – all at once – their little arm branches rose as if shaking their fists at the sky. Their trunks popped out of the ground, and they ran around in random directions.

Ethan and Hayley laughed as the small trees ran about the pen bumping into one another only to bounce off and continue in a different direction.

"Bumper cars," Ethan said.

Then, all at once, the nomads stopped and dug their trunks back into the ground. Happy with their new locations, their arm branches returned to their sides, and they sat silently.

"That was so cute," Hayley laughed.

"Quite a hoot," Mrs. Moongarden added. "As you can see, trembling nomads do not like being arranged in neat little rows." She winked at Ethan.

"Mrs. Moongarden – what came between Daavic and his brother?" Ethan asked.

"I'm not exactly sure," she said.

They approached a wall of foliage with a dark tunnel. Mrs. Moongarden led them inside.

"Have you heard the story of *Jack and the Beanstalk?*" Mrs. Moongarden asked.

"Yes," Ethan said. "Fee, fi, fo, fum – are you taking us to a giant that eats children?"

They approached the end of the tunnel.

"No, but I will show you the beanstalk."

They exited the tunnel, and Mrs. Moongarden pointed skyward.

Ethan and Hayley's heads tilted back as they gazed into the sky. The beanstalk was three car lengths in diameter at its base. Its frame formed from thousands of intertwined vines – like a column of spaghetti hanging from a giant fork in the sky.

"Disappears into the clouds," Hayley said.

"Lois is a skyclimber vine," Mrs. Moongarden explained. "The 'swirling fan' pattern on her leaves are like a fingerprint, no two skyclimbers display the same pattern."

"Has anyone ever climbed it?" Ethan asked.

"I was getting to that. The boys tried, even though I forbade it. They were dear boys, but they did have an eye for mischief."

"What happened?" Ethan asked.

"I caught them and went to fetch their mother. They climbed down and hid for hours. I suspect they found a good hiding spot in the ruins."

"Can you show us the ruins?" Hayley asked.

"Certainly, they're up ahead," Mrs. Moongarden replied.

"Did they get into trouble a lot?" asked Ethan.

"They caused their fair share of mischief," Mrs. Moongarden snickered. "Created the zebra and giraffe I'll have you know."

Ethan and Hayley looked at each other.

"The boys were each assigned a species for evolutioneer training. One day Damien found his white horse species had evolved into a zebra."

"Daavic, I bet," Ethan said.

"Indeed," Mrs. Moongarden said. "When Damien learned his brother was responsible, he evolved Daavic's species into a giraffe."

"How did Damien find out?" Hayley asked.

"They never spoke a word about it. Neither why Daavic chose to deceive his brother, nor how Damien found out. Something had come between them, but they never spoke of why."

The path ended at a brick walkway that encircled a grass area with a fountain at its center. Beyond the courtyard to the right, a picket fence surrounded another grassy area. A willow swayed in the breeze, partially obstructing the view of a statue of a young woman. To the left sat the ruins of a stone castle where only a crumbling tower with a dark entrance still stood.

"I've saved the best till last," Mrs. Moongarden said. "The dancing angels are my personal favorite." She led them to the center of the courtyard.

Six plants surrounded the fountain. They had pumpkin-sized leaves at the bottom and long branches that rose above the fountain. Wilted lumps of tree bark sat atop the stems like balled fists.

"Withering froo flowers?" Ethan asked.

"They are a relative of the withering froo," Mrs. Moongarden smiled. "But they only emerge under specific conditions, and fortunately, I control the Moongarden."

She pulled out her ELMO and tapped at the screen.

"First, they need water to play in," she said as a fine mist sprayed from the fountain. "Next, we'll need a full moon."

Day turned to night, and within minutes the silvery light of the moon filled the sky.

"And now – we wait."

Moments later, the gray lumps began to unravel into elegant angel-like wings. The stems were budding with activity as the angels exercised their delicate wings, and a brilliant yellow glow illuminated them internally. Then – one by one, they took off – the dance had begun.

The dancing angels were hypnotizing and resembled butterflies but were more graceful. Their motion was fluid as they swiftly danced above the mist, and the light illuminating their bodies cast a circular glow where their heads might be.

"They have halos," Ethan said, proud of his discovery.

"A dozen candied fox tails for you."

The angels danced in a circular formation above the mist. One of the angels broke away and swooped into the fog illuminating the water from within like a bird in a cage.

As the angel danced in its watery cage, something spectacular happened. Water droplets hitting the angel's body would sparkle and bounce off into a shimmering cascade of gold.

"Pixie dust," Hayley said as she held her hand out to catch some beneath the fountain.

"Gold dust," Ethan corrected Hayley.

"Dancing angels do attract their share of leprechauns," Mrs. Moongarden smiled.

One by one, the angels took turns showering gold dust into the fountain until it overflowed. When they finished, snow of gold covered the ground around the fountain. The dance ended when the last angel rejoined formation. They returned to their stems and withered into ugly lumps.

"That was awesome," Ethan turned towards Hayley – but she was gone.

"NO, Hayley! NO!" Mrs. Moongarden screamed. She tapped her ELMO and the daylight returned. Hayley held a colorful golf ball sized fruit as she knelt at a vine that poked from beneath a white picket fence.

Mrs. Moongarden ran towards Hayley, who had a crazed grin on her face as she rose. She arrived and in one swift motion, swatted the ball from Hayley's hand. Another slap across the face broke her from the spell.

"What happened?" Hayley asked.

"You were in a trance," Ethan said as he rushed to her side.

"This is most disturbing – you nearly ate a petrified wood berry," said Mrs. Moongarden. "I'm sure I removed the fruit and pruned back all the vines."

"What would happen if she ate that fruit?" Ethan asked.

"She'd petrify – like Pandora," Mrs. Moongarden pointed at the statue under the willow where a wooden figure of a woman holding an open box stood. She had a crazed grin as Hayley had, and leafy vines grew from her feet in all directions – Pandora was the vine.

"She was alive," Ethan said. Chills crept up his spine as he realized what almost happened to Hayley.

"Yes," Mrs. Moongarden replied. "A petrified wood berry is irresistible once touched. The victim is overcome by the urge to consume it, which leads to petrifaction, vine growth, and eventually fruit pods."

"Ethan, did you see where the fruit landed?" Mrs. Moongarden asked. "I must track it down."

"This is what you are looking for, I presume," Daavic said as he emerged from the tunnel holding the colorful fruit in his red gloved hand.

"I trust such carelessness will not happen again," Daavic said to Mrs. Moongarden as he tossed the deadly fruit into the fenced area.

"I took every precaution," Mrs. Moongarden said.

"Obviously not enough."

"I can't imagine how this happened, but I will get to the bottom of this."

"I hope you enjoyed the tour," she said to Ethan and Hayley. "I'm sorry it ended with such sour apples."

"I had a wonderful time," Hayley hugged Mrs. Moongarden.

"Me too," Ethan said as he hugged Mrs. Moongarden too.

"I have something to show our guests – you are excused," Daavic said.

Mrs. Moongarden choked back tears as she hurried into the dark tunnel.

THE SECRET WISHING WELL

First, I would like to apologize," Daavic said. "I've been on edge lately, and I've mistreated you."

Daavic's admission surprised them both.

"So, how do you like the Moongarden?" Daavic asked.

"Awesome," Ethan answered.

"I love it," Hayley agreed.

"My brother and I played here nearly every day – and do you know what we found?"

"What?" Ethan asked.

"Not even Mildred Moongarden understands all its secrets. Many years ago, my brother and I became bored with the Moongarden until my brother had an idea – to climb the skyclimber."

Ethan and Hayley gasped as they gazed skyward at the mammoth vine.

"We didn't make it far before Mrs. Moongarden caught us. She was livid and went to tell our mother. So, we climbed down and hid in the ruins. Nobody ever ventured into the ruins because of the stories."

They hung on Daavic's every word.

"Stories?"

"Tales that something haunts the ruins. We hid for hours before poking around inside, and then we discovered it."

"Discovered what?" Ethan asked.

"A secret wishing well, hidden right here in plain sight."

Ethan and Hayley scanned the area.

"But nothing is here," Hayley said.

"Would you like to see for yourself?"

They both nodded in agreement.

"Follow me," Daavic said with a grin.

Daavic led them towards the partially standing castle tower. Stones had crumbled away at the top, leaving a jagged and uneven surface. As they entered, their eyes took a moment to adjust to the dimly lit interior.

"As you may have realized, it is quite dark in here. So naturally, the surroundings spooked us after a few hours. We pried at the stones on the walls to let more light in – and then we found this."

Daavic pulled a stone from the wall, and a pink glow emanated from the exposed hole. He reached in and pulled out a moon-shaped rock that glowed in the dark. He held it up, and its pearly pink texture glistened in the darkness.

"We were surprised to find this. It has such an irregular shape. Where would you imagine it goes?"

Ethan remembered seeing the shape when they entered. It matched a hole in the wall where a stone was missing.

"Right there," he said and pointed at the hole where a column of light peaked into the room.

"The honor is yours," Daavic said and handed Ethan the rock.

Ethan slid the rock into place, and the surrounding wall flattened into a smooth square panel. Four concentric circles etched into the panel before their eyes, exposing a pink glow. Symbols appeared evenly spaced within the circular bands. It resembled a dartboard with rings of characters around a small arrow pointing up in the bullseye.

Ethan and Hayley exchanged glances. They had both seen that one of the four symbols in the innermost ring was Ethan's.

"What is that?" Hayley asked.

"A selection dial or lock of some kind. We only tried a few combinations before we hit pay dirt."

Daavic spun the dials and lined up certain symbols with the arrow at the center. The symbols blinked, and suddenly they were able to see clearly in the dark.

"I can see all of a sudden," Hayley said.

"Me too," Ethan said.

"Dark light is what Damien called it."

Ethan pointed to a previously invisible staircase spiraling up the inner walls of the structure.

"Those stairs weren't here before."

"Shall we?" Daavic said and motioned towards the foot of the staircase. There was no railing, so they ascended the narrow steps slowly. The dark light lit their way to the top, where they found a dark tunnel. Dark light did not work inside, but the light at the end of the tunnel guided them, so they rushed through and quickly emerged into daylight.

Ethan rubbed his eyes as they adjusted. "What the—"

"How did we end up here?" Hayley asked.

They were back in the courtyard as if they had just stepped out of the stone ruins. Everything looked the same yet different – a wishing well sat at the center where the fountain had been, and the ruins were gone.

"I present to you – the secret wishing well."

Ethan and Hayley ran to the well, and Daavic followed.

The wishing well was crafted from a pearly-pink material. Solid gold trim and an assortment of inlaid black diamonds decorated the shell. The pink structure glimmered in the sunlight and from some angles threw out cold bluish hues.

"How beautiful," said Hayley.

"Quite, but there is much more to appreciate. The water in this well has curative properties, which is why I brought you here." Daavic turned to Hayley and smiled. "The well can restore your memory."

Daavic turned the well's crank with his red gloved hand. Rope gathered on its spindle, and a small wooden bucket with a golden ladle emerged. Daavic scooped up some water and held it in front of Hayley's face.

"No, thank you," Hayley said as she pushed the ladle away with her hand.

Daavic put the oversized spoon back in the bucket. "Suit yourself."

"On second thought," Hayley said as she picked up the ladle and gulped down a scoop of water.

Ethan wanted to take a drink too but didn't.

"That was fantastic, but I feel strange," Hayley said with a devilish grin.

"It doesn't work right away," Daavic said as he lowered the bucket into the well.

"Daavic—" Ethan said. "Can you tell us about the Hybrid Child?"

Daavic pursed his lips and bowed his eyebrows as he considered Ethan's question.

"The Hybrid Child is an abomination. Ever since the Seers intervened – he's been an idealistic symbol of hope for the foolish—"

Ethan and Hayley looked at one another as silence filled the air.

"Come – we've stayed long enough – we don't want people to hear voices."

"How do we leave?" Hayley asked.

"Simply step outside the circle," Daavic said as he walked towards the edge of the courtyard.

Ethan sat at the edge of the well and stared inside.

Daavic reached the edge of the brick walkway, turned around, took a step backward, and vanished.

Hayley followed Daavic. "Where did he go?"

Ethan glanced up as Hayley disappeared. He started after her but then stopped.

"It is a wishing well," Ethan said to himself as he dug into his pocket, fished out a coin, and flipped it into the well.

"Ouch—" a voice said from within the well, and a fluttering sound echoed up the shaft.

"Ugggggggggggg . . ." the voice said.

Gruggins fluttered up from the well carrying the bucket and ladle – surprising Ethan. He set them on the edge of the well and landed on the bucket's rim.

"Found my secret napping hole," Gruggins said as he jumped onto the handle of the ladle.

"Daavic showed us," Ethan said. "He and Hayley just left."

"Daavic—" Gruggins grumbled. "He and Damien used to bother me too. I thought I had everybody scared off with the ghost stories till those two showed up."

"It was you – you were the voice of the haunted ruins."

"It was me all right," Gruggins laughed but then stopped. "Promise me you will keep my secret."

"I won't tell anybody," Ethan promised.

"Drink to it," Gruggins said. He slid down the handle of the ladle into the bucket and stopped by catching his feet on the lip.

"Always parched after a good nap," Gruggins said as he scooped up a handful of water and gulped it down. He hopped to the rim of the bucket and peered at Ethan. "Drink to it," he said and pointed into the bucket.

Ethan scooped himself some water and drank.

"You better go, but don't forget your promise," Gruggins said.

Ethan exited where he had seen Hayley disappear. He reappeared in the courtyard where Hayley and Daavic were waiting.

"What was the holdup?" Daavic asked.

"I had to tie my shoes," Ethan said.

"We heard voices," Daavic said.

"Oh, that – I was trying to spook Hayley."

Daavic bought Ethan's explanation and escorted them out of the Moongarden.

AN OCEAN OF TROUBLES

After their tour of the Moongarden, Ethan and Hayley headed back to their rooms. On their way, they reencountered Irvin.

"Shnickyrooners and shnackleboxes and things like that," Irvin jabbered as he appeared out of the darkness. "You ever notice that wherever winged skunk rats play in the muddy popsicle drippings of fresh beetle dung there is always a piece of white pound cake dancing with a smelly old weasel troll?"

"I've never noticed that, Irvin," Ethan said.

Irvin smiled at Ethan. "Got you a present I did, a present for Irvin's new friend." He reached into his jacket. "Ethan Fox liked Irvin's pocket tote . . . so Irvin got Ethan Fox his very own adventuring pack." Irvin handed Ethan a small yellow pouch.

"Thank you," Ethan said with excitement. He tugged at the small string on the pocket tote to make it grow and then at the other string to make it shrink.

"Ethan Fox is already an expert," Irvin said. "Now then, the Headmistress would like a word with Ethan Fox and Miss Hayley. She is awaiting your arrival in the Map Room."

Ethan and Hayley continued to the Map Room.

"Ethan, I don't think Daavic did that to help me. My ring told me not to drink, but when I touched the ladle – I couldn't stop myself."

"Daavic was a little too friendly," Ethan said.

"Yeah, at first – but then he seemed angry when you asked him about the Hybrid Child."

"He did seem angry – but he also helped confirm one thing."

"What's that?" Hayley asked.

"The Hybrid Child has a connection to the Seers – like me."

They arrived at the Map Room, and as they strode over the invisible floor, Ethan trod softly.

"Please – have a seat," Jordanna said as they reached the crow's nest. "I trust you had a pleasant time in the Moongarden."

"I loved the trembling nomads," Hayley said as she took a seat. Ethan sat down, as well.

"My Hayley loved the nomads too," Jordanna said.

A loud noise interrupted as alarms sounded, and the Map Room came to life. The lights dimmed as Jordanna eased back in her chair. Ethan and Hayley did the same. The crow's nest vanished, and a detailed map of the globe enveloped the room, and this time two red dots flashed on the world.

"Tell us what we're looking at," Jordanna said to no one in particular.

"Troubles in the Pacific," a voice answered.

Ethan observed as Jordanna spoke to the Map Room. He realized the room had intelligence and an understanding of Earth's every interaction.

"Connect me with Fin. Poseidon must be aware of this."

"Certainly," the voice replied.

An image appeared in midair – a holographic window into a control room. An amphibious humanoid creature studied charts spread out on a table, and then he looked up.

"Fin Drenchler here – we've been expecting your call. Disturbing events have occurred, and the humans are very alarmed."

Fin's deep navy-blue color glistened with yellow highlights, and his oversized orange eyes bulged from his frogish face. Fish-lips and scaly fin-like ears protruded from his head. He had long webbed hands, and his smooth, shiny skin appeared wet.

"Elaborate," Jordanna said.

"First we have this," Fin said. A new window appeared with a live feed from a human news channel:

"Shocked Washington beachgoers bore witness this morning as killer whales washed ashore by the dozens. The death toll is climbing steadily as whales continue to wash ashore. One hundred eleven at last count, but it is how they died that has experts baffled. Many of them bitten in half, it appears. It's no wonder locals here are talking of sea monsters."

The news camera panned the long stretch of beach, and as far as the eye could see, mangled orcas littered the beach. Many had deep wounds, and huge chunks of flesh ripped from their bodies. Jordanna gasped.

"This could only mean one thing," Fin said.

Hayley rubbed her ring finger and then spoke loudly. "The Outpost – Inner Island is in danger!"

"The girl knows something," Fin said.

"Indeed, she does," Jordanna said. "What do you know of Inner Island?"

"Nothing I can remember, but you have to believe me – it's never wrong."

Jordanna glanced at Hayley's ring that silently slithered around her finger. "Your ring?"

"Yes, it tells me things," Hayley said.

"May I?" Jordanna asked.

"It won't come off. It doesn't want to," Hayley said as she tugged at the ring, but it tightened around her finger.

"Leave it alone. If it is talking to you, there is a good reason. It may help unravel the mysteries of your past."

"If I may continue," Fin interrupted. "Grimleavers have compromised our communications, so I suggest a face to face meeting."

Jordanna agreed.

"I will send a bubble-pod at first sun," Fin said. "Our safest mode of transportation for land dwellers."

"Fine, and I will contact the Outpost."

Jordanna studied Ethan and Hayley as she pondered something.

"I will include our guests in the under-party. They may prove useful," she said.

The windows disappeared and broke off communication.

"Patch me through to Commander Triplin."

Another window appeared, a pale man in a Caretaker robe answered.

"Triplin here. How may I serve you, Headmistress?"

"Has anything out of the ordinary occurred?"

"Nothing – all has been quiet."

"Are all three accounted for?" she asked.

"I checked on them myself less than an hour ago."

"Report immediately if anything unusual occurs," Jordanna ended the communication.

"Anything else?" she said to the Map Room.

"We've received word from Alexander," the voice replied. "He is reporting of Grimleaver chatter that Victor Qruefeldt has become fearful . . ."

"Fearful of what?"

"He did not elaborate, but our spies have sent word that Victor has received a leap-letter."

The Map Room quieted, and Jordanna turned to Ethan and Hayley.

"You two should get some sleep. Tomorrow you're in for an adventure."

Ethan and Hayley adjourned to their rooms, but neither could sleep a wink.

"Ethan – can I come over?" Hayley ELMO'ed.

"Sure, I can't sleep either."

Ethan was at his desk with an old fashion pen and inkwell when Hayley arrived. He was writing his symbol all over his pocket tote.

"What are you doing?" she asked.

"Trying to keep my mind off tomorrow. Besides, now we know whose pocket tote it is."

Hayley laughed.

"I wonder what a leap-letter is," Ethan said. "The Map Room said that Victor Qruefeldt had received a leap-letter."

"Don't ask me how I know this, but a leap-letter is a telegram from the future."

"Who would be sending Victor a telegram from the future?"

"Could be anybody, even Victor himself," Hayley said.

Ethan put the inkwell on his dresser with his pocket tote. He sat on his bed with his back against the headboard.

"I wonder where we're going tomorrow," Ethan said.

"Who knows."

Hayley laid down and rested her head in Ethan's lap. They both fell fast asleep.

Morning came, and a knock on the door woke them – it was Brianna.

"Rise and sss-shine, I've come to gather you for our journey."

Brianna escorted them to the study where Jordanna and Daavic were waiting.

"Brianna and Daavic will accompany you," Jordanna said. "You will book-travel to *Tunnel Beach* where a team of Seakeepers will escort you to Poseidon."

"Book-travel?" Ethan asked.

"I forget, we have first-timers," Jordanna said. "Some books in this room are extraordinary." She walked to the bookcase nearest the fireplace. The books all appeared the same – withered brown books with gold lettering. Ethan noted a resemblance to the one his dad had hidden.

"The books on this shelf are portals, and today's journey begins here," Jordanna pulled one from the shelf and held it up so Ethan and Hayley could see.

Tunnel Beach

"*Tunnel Beach*," Brianna read aloud. "Been quite some time since I've journeyed to Poseidon."

"I've never been myself. Thank you for accepting my request, Mother," Daavic said.

"About time you've taken more initiative. Fin's team will meet you on *Tunnel Beach*. Poseidon is their domain, so follow their orders and respect protocol."

"You speak of protocol, yet taking humans to Poseidon is against protocol," Daavic said.

Brianna's tail fluttered like a rattler. "Sss-stop questioning your Mother's authority."

"You've always questioned authority," Jordanna said.

An uncomfortable silence filled the air.

CHAPTER ELEVEN

"Form a circle hand to shoulder – you must all be touching," Jordanna said as she handed the book to Brianna and stepped back.

"You may become sleepy but don't fight it."

Brianna opened the book and bright beams of light radiated from its pages. She stared into the light that shone on her face and snapped the book shut.

JOURNEY TO POSEIDON

Ethan woke up at the edge of a rainforest that nuzzled up against a secluded beach. Hayley sat in a patch of grass and watched as he slept.

"I thought you were never going to wake up," she said.

"Where are we?" Ethan asked as his arms raised and mouth stretched into a giant yawn.

"*Tunnel Beach* – don't you remember?"

Ethan struggled to his feet and studied his surroundings. The sight of Daavic and Brianna jogged his memory.

"The brown book—" Ethan said. "Hayley, my dad has a portal book that he keeps hidden in his office."

"We should tell Jordanna – we can trust her," Hayley said.

"She's not the one I'm worried about – Daavic is. Something's not right with him."

"I agree – I still can't believe I drank from that wishing well."

Brianna slithered towards them and cut their conversation short. Daavic held his ELMO up and gazed out to sea.

"They must have spotted something," Hayley said.

"Our boy is finally up?" Brianna asked as she smiled in her usual friendly manner. "First time is always the hardest, but you'll adjust."

"Have you spotted the Seakeepers?" Hayley asked.

"Yes – they'll be arriving shortly."

As they walked the beach, Ethan took in its beauty. They were on a fan-shaped beach with white sands that melted into the emerald waters. At each end of the beach, arms of foliage covered rock reached out to welcome the sea and form a broad cove.

"They're entering the shallows," Daavic said as they reached the water's edge.

Ethan scanned for signs of the approaching Seakeepers. Something had entered the cove and stirred up the water. There were several of them, making high arching leaps out of the water as they approached.

"Porpoises," Ethan said.

"Hydromorphs," Brianna corrected as five porpoises swam into the shallows and paused. They charged forward with the surf and beached themselves, the water receded, and the porpoises transformed. Their bodies rose from the wet sand as they morphed into humanoids.

"Sss-shape-shifters of the sea."

In humanoid form, hydromorphs displayed an impressive array of colors, each with a unique color scheme. Ethan recognized Fin Drenchler with his deep blue and yellow highlights.

"Welcome," Fin greeted the under-party as he walked onto the beach accompanied by two others. Two remained in the surf and alertly scanned the area. They were much larger than Fin and deep green with thick armored scales. They reminded Ethan of *The Creature from the Black Lagoon* — obviously Fin's security detail.

"I'd like you to meet my wife Lyn, and our son Gil."

Lyn was petite with floppy tadpole-like protrusions for ears. She had brilliant coloring like an underwater rainbow that appeared to Ethan like reef camouflage.

Gil was a mini-Fin with different colors — white with splotches of greens and blues and gold hints. He took an immediate liking to Hayley and smiled at her in a blatant display of affection.

"The bubble-pod will be arriving soon," Fin said.

A disturbance agitated the water as a hole formed several feet from shore. The gap grew more extensive and pushed towards the beach, forming two water walls that parted, creating a wet sandy walkway to a water tunnel.

"I will accompany you inside while my team swims along outside," Fin said as he motioned towards the tunnel.

"Might I swim along as well?" Brianna asked. "At least until we lose the light."

"Feel free. You can join us inside whenever you're comfortable."

Fin led them into the tunnel, where they entered a giant capsule of air. They stepped inside, and a firm buoyant surface met their feet like a giant waterbed.

"We'll walk to the nearest bubble port. The bubble port network is a series of depth portals we've installed. The depth drops off fast, so we won't need to travel too far."

As they walked along, the air capsule followed as they progressed deeper beneath the water's surface.

Crystal-clear water surrounded the bubble-pod and allowed them to view their surroundings. A beautiful underwater seascape with plant and animal life thrived in the tropical waters. Brianna's snake-like body adapted well to swimming underwater, so she and the Seakeepers swam alongside the protective bubble-pod. She looked like a cross between a mermaid and a giant sea snake.

The Seakeepers had transformed back into porpoises. Except for Gil, who had transformed into a boy in swimming trunks. Only his webbed hands and feet gave him away as he swam around outside the bubble-pod and performed stunts to gain Hayley's attention. Hayley finally took an interest as Gil motioned for her to come closer.

"What does he want?" Hayley asked.

As she approached, he blew bubbles from his nose, but instead of rising to the surface, the bubbles floated sideways and morphed into small seahorses.

"How cute," said Hayley.

"Big deal, they're just bubbles," Ethan whispered to himself.

Gil continued to blow bubbles in the shapes of fish, birds, whales, mermaids, and hearts that broke into smaller hearts.

"Enough flirting," Fin said to break up the fun. "We will be descending quickly from here."

Gil morphed into a porpoise and rejoined the others.

Brianna approached the exterior of the bubble-pod and pushed at the invisible barrier. She emerged inside like she was climbing out of a reverse water balloon – first one arm, then the other, followed by her head, body, and tail.

"Nothing like a refreshing swim."

Brianna dripped with water, but as each drop hit the floor, it absorbed back into the surrounding ocean.

They passed the edge of the underwater cliff, and the bubble-pod angled down like they were walking down an invisible staircase. As the light from the surface slowly vanished, the Seakeepers lit the way. Their bodies emitted a bright bluish glow that lit the bubble from the outside. Inside, Brianna provided light as the small tube-like worms on her head glowed a soft green.

They continued until they reached their destination. In the blackness of the deep, the team could hardly see, as bioluminescence didn't give off much light. What was visible as they got closer appeared to be a giant black cube that hung still in mid-water. It was much larger than the bubble-pod they were in. The Seakeepers disappeared beneath the cube and took their light with them. Everything got much darker as only Brianna's worm hair provided light.

The bubble-pod continued towards the cube on a collision course, but there was no collision when the time came. The bubble-pod melted into the cube, opening a hole in its side where a bright light shone through. The bubble-pod disappeared into the side of the giant cube taking the under-party inside with it.

They found themselves in a brightly lit room. The Seakeepers were already inside and in humanoid form. The cube appeared to be a furnished apartment with an instrument panel on one of the black walls.

"Bubble ports serve as remote quarters," Fin said as he walked to the instrument panel and hit buttons. "From here, we will take a series of slide tunnels. The bubble-pod is far too slow, so it will follow us down for your trip back."

The wall above the instrument panel came to life, and a giant map of tunnels appeared.

"The yellow line shows our path – only four depth portals away, but the changes in depth are extreme."

Fin punched one final button, and a broad tunnel appeared at the base of one of the walls. It resembled the bubble-pod they had arrived in, but a dim bluish glow lit the inside.

As they entered, the tunnel angled down at an increasingly steep incline until it became impossible to stand. The tunnel turned into a slippery slide as they zipped down its steep embankment. It was better than the wildest waterslide Ethan had ever been on. They slid for at least a minute before leveling off and ending at another bubble port.

They repeated the process three more times, each time journeying deeper into the abyss. As their slide down the final tunnel slowed, the blackness outside lightened. They rose to their feet and walked, and the tunnel grew brighter as they rounded a bend. The tunnel straightened, and a massive dome of light became visible, resting on the seafloor like a giant snow globe half-buried in the muck.

"What is that?" Hayley asked.

"An underwater city," Ethan said.

"Poseidon," said Daavic.

The tunnel curved towards the dome of light. When the team reached the light, there were no walls or barriers as Ethan had expected, only a dome of light encompassing the environment within. It was like walking from night into day with a single step. They were still inside a tunnel, only now it was brilliantly lit – like a tunnel inside a giant dome aquarium.

The surroundings reminded Ethan of a tropical coral reef, but this was much more spectacular. The visibility reached as far as their eyes allowed in the crystal-clear water. The golden sand on the ocean floor was the perfect canvas for the abundant sea life to glide above like an artist's brush. An assortment of creatures swam overhead. Giant seahorses swam outside the tunnel and were nearly big enough to saddle. Schools of V-shaped rays gracefully swam in perfect formation and turned in unison.

"I've never seen these types of sea creatures, and I watch a lot of Discovery Channel," Ethan said.

"No human ever has," Daavic said.

"Mermaids," Hayley said as she pointed to a group of three that gracefully swam by.

"Hydromorphs, actually," Fin corrected. "We often took merman and mermaid form when we first arrived in Earth's oceans, but several unfortunate human sightings convinced us of better options."

"How much farther to Poseidon?" Daavic asked.

"I thought this was Poseidon," Hayley said.

"Poseidon is over there," said Gil as he pointed and smiled at Hayley.

The tunnel angled down an incline, giving them a view through the ceiling above. Ethan gazed up at Poseidon, and it took his breath away.

Poseidon sat half embedded into the side of a seamount. The shimmering palace had been carved from an enormous pink pearl that was still partially intact. The palace structure appeared unfinished, but that was part of its allure. The spherical surface of the pearl abruptly ended where the palace began. It looked like someone had cracked open a giant round egg and erected a pink castle inside.

The tunnel ended at the base of a steep set of stairs that led to the palace. Many grueling moments later, they arrived at the top of the staircase. They found themselves in a foyer that led to a much larger room. The inside of the palace was as breathtaking as the outside. The doors, tables, chairs, staircases, and support columns were all sculpted from the polished pink pearl as if the entire palace were a single carved piece.

They entered a room with high ceilings and a grand staircase that fanned out at the bottom and forked at the top. Tall spiral columns decorated the interior from floor to ceiling like the inside of a giant seashell.

"Given the situation, we will start immediately," Fin said. "Please, follow me."

Fin led them through double doors to the right of the staircase. They entered the room and found the Seakeeper briefing team waiting. They sat at a pearlescent pink boardroom table, which was sculpted up from the polished floor.

Fin introduced his team, Brooke Troutland, and Marlin Trollwell.

Brooke was petite like Fin's wife, but her colors were more feminine with subdued pinks and whites, with magenta highlights that looked like lipstick. Brooke was in charge of the Pacific Ocean detail.

Marlin was Fin's right hand man. He coordinated Seakeeper operations, monitored human communications, and reported to Fin. Taller and thinner than the other Seakeepers, Marlin appeared to be a different species. He had long arms and legs and bigger webbed hands and feet. His head resembled a long smooth teardrop that forked at its tail end.

Everyone took a seat at the table. Ethan took out his pocket tote and fumbled it from hand to hand as he waited. He gazed around the room and spotted Fin staring at his pocket tote, then their eyes met.

"Ethan Fox, I've been hearing a lot about you," Fin said. "Would you stick around after the briefing so that we can chat?"

"Sure."

"Great – enough small talk, let's get started," Fin said. "First, we must take precautions." Fin held up an ELMO and scanned everyone in the room.

"What is the meaning of this?" Daavic protested.

"You will understand once we have briefed you," Fin said.

"Over the last two days, disturbing events have occurred," Marlin said. "Brooke will report the details."

A broad map appeared on the wall.

"The first event took place here," Brooke said and pointed to a flashing red dot. "Two days ago, a U.S. Naval submarine went missing. We intercepted their distress signal. The Navy has launched a search for their missing sub."

"Humans are always losing their naval ships," Brianna said.

"We located and cloaked the sub, but our findings are alarming. The hull was shredded down its entire length. Sadly, there were no survivors."

"No earthly creature could do such a thing," Brianna said.

"Exactly," said Fin.

"The second event occurred here, where it fed on a superpod of orcas," Brooke said as she pointed to a second dot.

"It can't be—" Brianna gasped.

"It can only be," Fin insisted. "They've released a kraken!"

"We have accounted for all three pups," Daavic said.

"Yet the evidence remains, only a kraken could cause such destruction. And there is more – we've tracked it to the *Mariana Trench* and discovered a series of tunnels."

Hayley rubbed her ring as it slithered on her finger. "It is searching for something – I warned you about the Outpost. Something is wrong!"

The room fell silent as everyone turned to Hayley.

"Indeed, you did, and I'm beginning to agree," Fin said.

Daavic shifted in his seat and appeared irritated at Hayley's participation.

"How do Grimleavers figure into this?" Daavic asked.

"That involves other unfortunate events and an old Seakeeper secret," Fin sighed. "Many years ago, when Ryvias was Headmaster, a Seakeeper named Newt Dripmore went missing."

"I recognize that name," Daavic said.

"I was the new leader of the Seakeepers, handpicked by Ryvias himself. I had reason to suspect foul play, so I decided to share our secret with Ryvias. A secret no Seakeeper had ever shared before – but I am about to share with you. Hydromorph blood is transmorphic."

"Transmorphic – no wonder you've kept that a sss-secret."

"What is transmorphic?" Ethan asked.

"It means if Victor Qruefeldt ever got his hands on a hydromorph – he would have the means to create an army of sss-shape-shifting vampires."

"Not exactly," Marlin said. "The effects wear off after a couple of hours. Regardless, this is not a weapon we want the Grimleavers to acquire."

"Which is exactly why I told Ryvias, I had a missing hydromorph – and there was a good chance the Grimleavers had learned our secret. I had to tell the Caretakers."

"Then why are we only learning of this now?" Daavic asked.

"Newt Dripmore was never found, and the Seakeeper secret died with Ryvias. We couldn't risk telling anyone else – until now."

"And how does this relate to current events?" Daavic asked.

"Two more hydromorphs have gone missing," Fin said. "Sal and Sil Finley, a husband and wife team. The Grimleavers have learned our secret – there is no question in my mind."

"Well, that explains the precautions," Brianna said. "We must return to The Residence immediately – we must tell the Headmistress of this news."

"The bubble-pod will not arrive for hours," Marlin said.

"Anything else to report?" Fin asked.

"We've received word from the field," Brooke said. "Our sources are reporting more of the same – the Grimleavers are worried that we will unlock the portals."

"If we have nothing else," Marlin said. "We will provide you quarters until the bubble-pod arrives. If you are hungry, a mess hall is close by. We have updated your ELMOs with maps of the palace."

The map on the wall disappeared, and the briefing was over.

"I will show you to your quarters," Marlin offered as he ushered everyone out of the briefing room.

Ethan stuck around after the briefing as Fin had asked. Their talk only lasted a few minutes, so Ethan used the ELMO palace map to find the way to his room. Along the way, he spotted Daavic sneaking down a hallway. Ethan was curious where Daavic was going, so he peeked at his ELMO map. Daavic was heading down the storage vault hallway, but when Ethan peeked down that corridor – Daavic was gone.

Ethan arrived at his quarters, and as expected, it was a replica of his bedroom at home; but now he had a waterbed. Hayley's room was next to his, so he knocked on her door. She answered and invited him in.

"What did Fin want?" Hayley asked.

"He was curious about the symbols on my pocket tote and wanted to know where I learned of Creator Stravis' symbol."

"You didn't tell him, did you?"

"Not exactly. I told him I had seen it on the spine of a book. But where have I heard that name before – Stravis."

"From Jordanna, when she said they learned of the Seers existence after unearthing Stravis' journal."

"Right, I remember now."

"Ethan, I have something to tell you. My ring has been teaching me—"

A knock at the door interrupted their talk. It was Brianna asking if they wanted to join her for lunch. They were both hungry, so they adjourned to the mess hall and shared a seafood tower. After lunch, the bubble-pod arrived, and it was time to go.

A DAMIEN
SIGHTING

Upon their return, Brianna and Daavic rushed to brief Jordanna. Hayley returned to her room while Ethan decided to peruse the study for more research. Ethan was in the study for only a minute when his ELMO woke up.

"Ethan, I need to show you something. Are you ready?"

"Ready for what?"

Ethan's ELMO transformed into a small metallic cat. And in a flash, he was face-to-face with Hayley in her pink-walled bedroom – and she was holding two ELMOs.

"How did you do that?"

"I've been practicing. My ring has been teaching me how to use the copycat. It is capable of a lot of things. I don't even have to be in the same room or in view of what it copies. As long as I can envision the object, I can make a copy."

"But how did I end up here?"

"The copycat can teleport things too. And if I want, it can bring back anything or anyone touching the item."

"You should call it a swappy-cat," Ethan said with a smirk.

"Yeah, I guess," she laughed. "It can remember things too. Watch this—"

Hayley wiggled her pinky finger, and the copycat Ethan held turned into Gruggins' green box. Another wiggle of her pinky and it turned into a girl's hairbrush.

"It remembers the forms it had taken before," Hayley's face turned serious. "But here's where things get creepy. You might want to set it down."

Ethan set the copycat on the floor. Hayley wiggled her pinky, and this time the copycat turned into a small hairy creature about six inches tall. A small black gorilla-like creature with long hair, saber-like teeth, and piercing red eyes glared up at them.

The animal leaped on Hayley's bed and growled.

"That is a grindle," Hayley said, then she twitched her pinky, and the copycat returned.

"That creature was alive. I thought it only copied inanimate objects."

"Me too. Those were some shapes the copycat remembers. I don't think Jordanna's Hayley was the original owner."

"Jordanna said Irvin gave her the copycat," Ethan said. "Maybe it was Irvin's."

"Not Irvin – whoever owned it knew you."

"I don't understand," Ethan said.

"I haven't shown you yet," Hayley said. She wiggled her pinky, and a holographic image appeared in midair: the scene of a small cabin in the woods, where a man in a Caretaker robe stood on the porch with two boys. A teenage boy had his hand on the shoulder of a much younger boy – Ethan Fox appeared to be about five years old in the image.

Ethan gasped in disbelief.

"You had a brother," Hayley said.

"He's not my brother – he's my dad – George Fox."

Hayley's eyes widened.

"I wonder who the man is," Ethan said as he studied the scene. "Hayley – we need to talk to Irvin and find out who owned the copycat."

Hayley agreed, but they decided not to tell Irvin about the copycat's secrets. Instead, they would bring it up in casual conversation. Ethan touched the "Irvin App" on his ELMO.

"Shnickyrooners and things like that," Irvin said. "Butterfly trolls always meet their doom on the bald head of a flaming water hippo, and they never even get to lick the rosy lizard dew from the field of dripping rock monkeys."

"I saw that on the Discovery Channel," Ethan replied.

"Irvin McGillicutty at your service."

"Hi, Irvin – Hayley and I were wondering if you needed help delivering your newspapers today?"

"No one has ever offered to help Irvin before."

"I can't believe that," Ethan said. "You mean the pesky butterfly trolls don't help you cook the pickled whisker mushrooms?"

Ethan's double-talk perked Irvin up.

"Thank you, Ethan Fox. Irvin has made his delivery today. But if you'd like to come to Market Square – you can help me shop for Moonflowers."

"We'd love to help," Ethan said.

They met Irvin in The Hall of Doorways at the tenth door on the right. They followed a winding yellow brick road that led to Market Square. Along the way, Hayley pulled out her copycat and stroked it.

"Miss Hayley likes the copycat? The Headmistress told me she was happy her Hayley's copycat chose you."

"I adore it, but I think it may be broken."

She held the statuette up in her left hand, and it turned into Gruggins' green box, and then into a cat, and then the box, and then the cat . . . Hayley wiggled her pinky behind her back to fool Irvin.

"I hoped you could tell us where you got it, so I can have it fixed."

"Irvin purchased the copycat at Market Square. Irvin will speak with the merchant, the blistering hogwart of a scoundrel will fix the copycat."

Market square was around the next bend – an enormous flea market in the middle of a town square. Masses of people gathered around produce, and fruit stands, and tents filled with all sorts of goodies. A mix of humanoids and non-humanoids were present, bartering, and bidding on items from the merchants.

The town surrounded the market like a colossal U. Only the yellow brick road led in or out. Shops and cafes dotted the inner edges of town. Irvin bought Ethan and Hayley each a sugar-pickle soda and led them to a small courtyard.

"Sit tight while Irvin finds that scoundrel."

Ethan and Hayley sat at a table outside a small cafe. They sipped their drinks, watching Irvin until he got a safe enough distance away for them to follow.

"Sugar-pickle soda sounds nasty but tastes awesome," Ethan said as he glanced away from Irvin. "Hayley – isn't that Daavic – sitting with those two creatures?"

"Looks like him, and those are forest trolls. I wonder what he's doing here?"

Daavic sat across Market Square from Ethan and Hayley at a sister cafe. He was in deep discussion with the trolls, and they were laughing.

"They sure are laughing it up," Hayley said.

"Maybe that's Damien, and those are his wives," Ethan said.

"E-E-Ethan – it isn't Damien – Damien is right there."

Hayley's hand trembled as she pointed a few tables over. Damien sat intensely focused on his brother. Ethan and Hayley sat motionless and watched Damien watch Daavic. Damien snapped out of it and jumped to his feet, then he paused and turned to wink at Ethan before rushing off into the crowd.

"Ethan – we should tell Daavic!"

But when they turned towards Daavic, he was gone, and so were the trolls.

In all the excitement, they failed to follow Irvin – but that didn't matter because the scoundrel merchant had left town.

Irvin was sad, but Hayley convinced him that she had fixed her copycat. She showed him that it no longer exhibited strange behavior. They spent the next hour helping Irvin shop for Mrs. Moongarden – Irvin was grateful.

THE CRITTER

After delivering the items to Mrs. Moongarden, Ethan and Hayley said their goodbyes. Irvin was so happy he morphed into a giant smile to show how his new friends made him feel.

They headed back to the study to continue their research. Daavic sat at the desk near the candelabrum when they entered. He stopped what he was doing and locked something away in the desk drawer. Whatever he was doing was for his eyes only.

"To what do I owe the pleasure?" Daavic said.

"We thought we would browse the library if you don't mind," Hayley replied.

"Certainly – just stay clear of the portal books. We wouldn't want you to end up in a dark hole somewhere."

Daavic left the study. Hayley scanned the regular shelves, but Ethan made a beeline for the portal books.

"Ethan – we've been warned not to go near that shelf."

"Don't worry – I'm not going to touch anything."

Ethan studied the gold lettering on the spines and whispered the titles: *Frosthaven Gully, Nimble Narrows, The Straits of Borealis* . . .

Hayley joined him and read from eye-level down while he proceeded upwards. He reached the upper shelves and could no longer read the titles, so he used the nearby bookshelf ladder.

"Strange – the titles on the top shelf are written in symbols like on the secret panel in the Moongarden's ruins – and a book is missing."

Hayley looked up at Ethan. "Ethan – come down before you fall."

Ethan climbed down, and they returned to the regular bookshelves to browse more titles. The door slammed shut and interrupted them – Daavic was not in a good mood.

"I'll be needing the study – please run along."

They exited the study, and the front room was quiet. Hayley approached Gruggins' box.

"Gotcha!" Gruggins growled as he popped out of his box and scared Hayley half to death. "Oops, I'm sorry, my dear – hope I didn't frighten you."

"You didn't. I just wanted to ask you—"

"Been sensing a critter on the loose," Gruggins interrupted. "I thought it was a tribe of Nibblewarts the first time I sensed it. Passed through this room a moment ago, so keep your eyes open and holler if anything catches your eye." Gruggins disappeared back into his box.

"That mirror has moved again," Ethan said.

Hayley approached the giant mirror to investigate. It now stood against the staircase.

"Ethan – my reflection – that isn't what I look like. Is it?"

Ethan joined Hayley in front of the mirror. He was the same, but Hayley was a different girl with dark brown hair, and her infinity ring was giving off a faint glow.

"You don't look anything like that – but I have an idea of what's going on."

"What?"

"Do you remember when we met Gruggins? He said 'it' was cloaking you for a reason. I think your ring is cloaking your real identity."

Hayley held up her hand and peered at her ring. She tugged at it, and this time it slipped off easily – and Hayley's reflection changed.

"There you are," Ethan said and smiled.

Hayley stood in front of the mirror, taking her ring on and off watching her reflection change. Ethan wandered to the base of the staircase.

"I wonder what's up there," he said and started up the stairs.

"Ethan – don't go up there."

She tried to stop him, but he was halfway to the next floor already. He continued to the second floor and glanced around as he stood atop the first flight of stairs.

"Ethan – come back down here now!"

"A hallway there," he said and pointed to the right. "A huge dark room straight ahead, and another room over here." Ethan walked into the room to his left.

"ETHAN!"

She could hear him talking to someone.

"How'd you get here? You were just—" Ethan fell silent.

"Gruggins! Something's happened to Ethan!" Hayley cried out at the top of her lungs.

Gruggins emerged from his box and fluttered over to Hayley. He rode on her shoulder as she ascended the stairs.

"I won't let any critter harm Ethan Fox," Gruggins comforted her.

They entered the room and found Ethan on the floor unconscious. Hayley rushed over and knelt beside him. Gruggins hopped on Ethan's chest and examined his feet, hands, side, and backside after Hayley helped flip him over.

"Curious – that explains a few things," Gruggins said as he stuffed something into his pocket.

"What's wrong with Ethan?"

"Don't worry, he'll be okay – sleepy but okay," Gruggins said with a smile. He hopped onto Hayley's shoulder and produced a blowgun out of thin air. "This will wake him up long enough to get him to his room." Gruggins blew into the blowgun, a dart zipped out the end and landed squarely in Ethan's shoulder – he began to stir.

"Gruggins—" Hayley said.

"Yes, my dear."

"Do you know who I am?"

"Of course, but don't worry yourself – I won't tell a soul. It is cloaking your identity for a reason."

"I—" Hayley's words froze.

"You should tell your mother. The Headmistress has never stopped searching."

"Jordanna – Jordanna is my mother?"

Tears streamed down both sides of Hayley's face.

"You didn't know?" Gruggins said. "If I would have known—"

"You said it is cloaking me for a reason," Hayley interrupted as she stroked her ring. "We must keep this a secret, for now. I will tell my mother when the time is right."

"Agreed," Gruggins said. "I'm happy to have you back, Miss Hayley. I've missed you."

Ethan finally came around and was groggy when he woke up, but he couldn't remember anything. The trip back to his quarters went fast with Hayley's help. She draped his arm over her shoulder and acted as a crutch while Gruggins rode along for moral support. They plopped him into bed, and Ethan was out like a light.

A GIFT FROM

JASPER

Ethan could hardly see in the blistering sandstorm. He pushed forward as if guided by an invisible force. He had the strange feeling he was being watched, but that was not possible under such conditions. Ethan continued onward as the winds subsided. The heat from the sun made its presence felt, and soon the wind had stopped completely.

Ethan stood in a vast desert surrounded by tall dunes of sand. He scanned his surroundings and saw what was watching him. Deep blue eyes, thousands of them peeked out from the dunes of sand. They did not frighten Ethan but instead calmed him.

"Who are you? Why am I here?" He tried to communicate with them, but the desert was still.

A disturbance caught Ethan's attention as a sizable hatch slowly swung open from beneath the sand. A man emerged from within the desert bunker. He was tall and wore a hooded yellow robe. He strode across the sand, oblivious to Ethan or the eyes in the desert sand. The man knelt to pick up a brown book with gold symbols that shimmered in the sun.

A bright flash blinded Ethan, and he was abruptly somewhere else. A swift breeze blew back his hair and whistled through the branches of a nearby willow tree. Dirt with patches of crabgrass covered the ground on which the man in the yellow robe lie dying. He was older now, and blood from deep wounds pooled beneath his body.

A three foot tall blue bunny approached, walking upright, and knelt to hug the dying man. The man reached into his robe, pulled out the brown book, and handed it to the bunny as he took his last breath. Yellow spots appeared on the bunny's blue fur as it cried at the man's side. Ethan recognized Jasper and tried to get his attention, but words would not leave his mouth.

Another bright flash and Ethan was standing in his bedroom at home. Jasper held the brown book out to Ethan and pleaded for him to take it. A shadow on the wall caught Ethan's attention – someone was behind him, but he could not move. The shadow grew taller as it approached Ethan from behind. The tall devilish figure with thick swooping horns moved closer – Victor Qruefeldt was behind him.

Ethan burst out of bed and tried to catch his breath as sweat poured from his forehead. He pulled back the sheets to wipe his brow and found something. Under the covers lying near the foot of his bed sat a withered brown book with golden symbols. Ethan didn't understand, had his nightmare been real?

Ethan was still in shock from his dream. He reached for the ELMO on his dresser and realized that his pocket tote was larger than he had left it. Someone had opened it and was snooping in his room.

"Hayley, I need to speak with you."

"Finally, I have something to tell—"

"Hayley!" Ethan interrupted. "Come over now."

His tone must have alarmed her because she arrived in a flash. He explained his nightmare in every detail.

"It was only a dream," Hayley consoled Ethan. "Probably just a side effect from the dart Gruggins woke you up with."

"Hayley, I'm not finished. When I woke up, I found this," he said as he held the book up.

"That appears to be a portal book. How did it get here?"

"Beats me – but someone's been snooping in my pocket tote too."

"Do you think it could be the missing book?" Hayley asked as she rubbed her infinity ring.

"I can't be sure – but I'm not going to open it." Ethan set the book in his lap. "Your ring talking again?"

"Something is about to happen," she said.

The book came to life as the cover flipped open. The yellowish pages glowed as they flipped from page to page like a card dealer shuffling cards. When it finished, the book sat in Ethan's lap opened to page one.

"Ethan, the poem – The Eyes of the Desert Sand."

The opened book had not transported them anywhere, so Ethan flipped through the pages.

"The pages are blank," Hayley said.

"All but the first one, it looks like there were other pages, but someone ripped them out."

Wisps of yellowish light wafted from the book's pages and disappeared in wavy clouds of golden smoke. Ethan pulled his hands away as the book took over. The pages flipped forward then back as if searching for a specific page before settling on the first blank page. Writing appeared at the bottom as if written by an invisible author. Another poem was being written backward:

Cruel Intentions

He lurks in shadows to hide from the light,
With cruel intentions he feeds on fright.

An evil plan with dreams so dire,
The Silent Forest will burn with fire.

To find the key things must unfold,
At a Grumpling's feet a secret is told.

Four portals locked away so tight,
Unlock the door to begin the fight.

In evil deception the path will be laid,
through the back door the toll will be paid.

"Silent Forest—" Ethan said.

"Ethan," Hayley interrupted. "My name is Hayley Ravenwood – I am Jordanna's daughter."

Ethan's jaw dropped open. "But – how?" he said. "Jordanna's Hayley went missing one hundred years ago."

"I don't know how – but I bet it has something to do with this rift-key."

"How did you find out?"

"Gruggins – I asked him to keep my secret. And I would tell my mother."

"What are we going to do about this?" Ethan asked and pointed to the poem that had just appeared.

"I think we should talk to my mother about this – but I have to tell her the truth first."

"I have a feeling that she already knows," Ethan said.

A GALLERY OF MEMORIES

Ethan woke up bright and early. Someone slipped a note under his door. As he pulled the message from the envelope, a fragrant scent reminded him of Jordanna. The note read:

Dear Ethan,

We've made little progress in discovering why you were lured to The Residence. A new discovery has been brought to my attention that we should discuss. Please gather Hayley and meet me in the front room. I have something to show you.

Sincerely yours,

Jordanna Ravenwood

Ethan ELMO'ed Hayley.

"Jordanna sent me a message and wants us to meet her in the front room."

"Good, I'd like you to be present when I tell her."

They entered the front room, and Jordanna was standing next to the giant mirror that had moved again – this time to the right of the front door.

"That was fast. I'm pleased you rushed," Jordanna said with a smile.

"Your note sounded important," Ethan said.

"Please, follow me," Jordanna said.

"Wait—" Hayley said. "First, I need to show you something."

Hayley slowly approached her mother. A tear peeked out from the corner of Jordanna's eye as Hayley neared and slowly slid her infinity ring off her finger. Tears streamed from Jordanna's eyes as she fell to her knees and hugged her daughter.

"My Hayley – you haven't aged a day," Jordanna cried. "I suspected you were my daughter, but I couldn't risk exposing you. There were too many coincidences, but you've been cloaked for a reason."

Ethan wiped his wet cheeks as he witnessed the tearful reunion. Hayley and her mother embraced for several minutes before regaining their composure.

"Now then," Jordanna said. "We must keep this a secret until we know why this ring is cloaking you."

"That isn't a ring – it's a rift-key," Ethan said.

"Rift-key—" Jordanna repeated. "That would explain the time jump and cloaking ability."

Hayley put it back on her finger, and her reflection changed again.

"But – I still see my Hayley."

"It no longer regards you as a threat," Hayley said.

"Well then," Jordanna said with a smile. "Let us move on to matters at hand – follow me."

She opened the door to the left of the front door. A cool breeze rushed by and gave Ethan the chills. They followed a dark hallway that curved right. There were no lights or windows, but the light from the end of the hallway shone their way.

They emerged into an enormous room with very high ceilings and scaffolding around its outer edges. The place resembled a brightly lit aircraft hangar with white canvas walls that ascended eighty feet straight up. Hundreds of paintings randomly hung scattered along the walls like postage stamps. A small elf-like creature hung from a rope in front of each painting.

"Welcome to our Gallery," Jordanna said. "The Gallery catalogs happenings past and present."

A portly elf waddled up to greet them. He wore a black suit jacket with worn blue jeans and red sneakers. Much older than the rest, he had gray hair and round glasses perched upon his long-pointed nose.

"This is our curator, Dorkin Drumbles," Jordanna introduced. "Most of our gallery workers are forest elves, uniquely adapted for hanging in trees – we'd have a difficult time otherwise."

"Help out we do," Dorkin had a quirky voice that reminded Ethan of Yoda. "Monitor the artwork, collect and mount for display, a crucial task it is."

Ethan scanned the enormous room as the elves cut finished pieces from the walls and collected them. The cutaway canvas magically grew back like a healing wound. Many of the paintings were still being painted – by invisible artists. Next to each unfinished piece, an elf hung from a rope and patiently held a palette of paint. Floating brushes magically dabbed at the palette and painted on the enormous canvas.

"Take finished pieces we do – for determination," Dorkin said as he motioned towards the floor area.

Two areas divided the floor, and in one, a team of elves mounted finished works into frames. In the other, elves placed finished works on easels while three old hags hunched over and studied them.

"The Fates determine significance," Jordanna said and pointed to the old hags. "If deemed important, we move them to the viewing hall. Otherwise, we catalog and store them away."

"Who is creating the paintings?" Ethan asked.

"We do not know, but we have never questioned the validity of a piece's significance."

"Why I sent for you it is, significant the new painting is."

They walked to a corridor at the far side of the room. The viewing hall had hundreds of paintings on its walls. Small spotlights brightly lit each image. They were in no particular order but were all framed and engraved with a caption at the bottom.

As they continued, something grabbed Ethan's attention. A painting of a desert landscape with blue eyes peeking out from within the dunes. They were watching a man in a yellow robe hunched over a baby bundled in a blanket and laying in the sand. A hatch lay open behind the man exposing a staircase descending into the sand – the entrance to a desert bunker.

They rounded a bend, and the paintings stopped, and only blank walls continued into the distance. Dorkin pointed at the last painting in the hall that was covered by a sheet.

"This one it is," Dorkin trembled with excitement.

Jordanna unveiled the painting of Ethan and Hayley on the boardwalk the moment they had first spotted one another. Ethan held his hand up to block the sun while Hayley looked back at him.

"I don't understand. We've already been through that," Hayley said.

"It isn't always obvious at first. Inspect the scene. Does anything appear out of place?"

"Him – that man is watching Ethan."

"Indeed, he is," Jordanna said.

The man sat on a bench with his hands in the pockets of his brown trench coat. He wore a black wide-brimmed hat and dark sunglasses.

"That day was warm. Nobody in their right mind would have worn a coat," Ethan said.

"Do you think he's a Grimleaver?" Hayley asked.

"Possibly, but they rarely venture into the human world," Jordanna said.

"They did the first time," Ethan said.

"Yes, they did." Jordanna agreed.

They stared at the painting for several more minutes, but nothing new came to mind, so they adjourned back to the front room.

THE FOUR PORTALS

Jordanna sat in a chair next to the spider-legged table in the room's center, and Hayley sat across from her. The phantom bubble hung motionless above the table. Ethan studied the narrow black carpet that ran from the front door to the marble slab against the far wall. A smile formed on his face as his eyes followed the rug to the front door – curiosity got the best of him.

"If this is the front room," he said as he approached the door, "then what's in the front yard?" Ethan yanked the door open, and a bright light shone into the front room as he and Hayley's eyes grew wide in surprise.

A black and white checkerboard plane stretched in all directions like an endless tiled floor. The blue sky appeared vibrant in the bright sun – yet no sun was visible. Giant dead trees lined the horizon, and their leafless limbs reached towards the sky as if in agony. Four colored metallic spheres hovered several feet above the checkered plane.

"What are those?" Ethan asked as he pointed at the basketball-sized orbs.

"They are portals," Jordanna said.

The four spheres hovered side by side in a row, each held in place by an electric field of a matching color: one red, one green, one blue, and one yellow. The electric fields emanated from beneath the checkered plane and blasted up like colorful bolts of lightning.

"Portals to where?" Ethan asked. "I'm going to take a closer look." Ethan stepped through the doorway, but he didn't make it far. His body reflected into The Residence as if he had just walked in from outside.

"You've discovered the lock, and it appears to be still working," Jordanna said. "Let me demonstrate." A rubber ball appeared in her hand, and she tossed it through the doorway. The ball disappeared for a second and then zipped right back in as if thrown from the other side.

"They've locked the doorway to the four portals so no one can use them," Jordanna said.

The bright sunless day outside lit the front room as colored beams of light reflected off the metallic spheres and created a pattern that danced along the carpet. Ethan studied the curious pattern as he closed the door.

"Those spheres are portals to the elemental worlds of the Chrysalis. Atlantis, Ceres, Hades, and Zephyr – our home worlds."

"Caretakers are aliens?" Ethan asked.

"More like distant cousins – the elemental worlds are a coalition of planets united under the Chrysalis."

"Chrysalis?" Hayley questioned.

"The Chrysalis is the energy that surrounds the elemental worlds and shields them and any planet under our protection. Earth is currently under such protection."

"Why would Earth need protection?" Ethan asked.

"To make a long story short, The Destroyer – evil's ultimate. When The Designer finished his greatest design, he needed a world to house them. So, he called upon our Council of Elders to select four Creators. Each elemental world chose one – Driveous, Vraitor, Zamalador, and Stravis."

Ethan was beginning to understand – the emblem on their robes – the candelabrum – the red, green, blue, and yellow. All representative of the four elemental worlds of the Chrysalis.

"The portals are created as a side effect when we pull a finished planet into the Chrysalis – they serve to transport us to and from the elemental worlds. Upon extraction, the portals serve a different purpose."

"Why lock them?" Ethan asked.

"In Earth's case, a Great Exodus occurred, and creatures from our worlds migrated here in vast numbers. The Creators returned to fix the situation and prevent a repeat; the Creators locked the portals when they left. The lock will only open upon discovery of the portal prophecies as written in the Book of Creators."

"What are the portal prophecies?" Hayley asked.

"For the lack of a better term, they are a countdown if you will. A series of events will occur, and when the last of them has come to pass, we must perform 'The Ritual of the Pyrodevlins' or the Chrysalis will perish."

Hayley gasped at the thought, but Ethan remained silent as he retrieved his pocket tote and tugged at its string to make it grow.

"Mrs. Ravenwood, the portal books in the study, why do the ones on the top shelf have symbols instead of letters?"

"Someone's been snooping," Jordanna said as she smiled at Ethan. "The books on that shelf are extraordinary. The symbols are from the secret language of the Creators. I can't read what is on those books – no Caretaker can."

"Mrs. Ravenwood – the Silent Forest is in danger."

Jordanna smirked at Ethan's mention of the Silent Forest. "And what would you know of the Silent Forest?" she asked.

Jordanna listened closely as Ethan described his scary dream. Ethan reached inside his pocket tote. "I woke up soaked in sweat, so I pulled back the sheets, and I found this—" Ethan held up the book for Jordanna, and its golden symbols glowed in the dim light of the front room – Jordanna gasped.

"We thought it might be the missing book from the top shelf," Hayley said.

"May I?" Jordanna asked.

Ethan handed the book to Jordanna, but the symbols faded away as soon as it left his hands, leaving only the worn brown cover. Jordanna studied the book and gently flipped through the pages but then stopped.

"No, this is not the missing portal – but it is curious."

She handed the book back to Ethan. Once in his grasp, the golden symbols returned to the book's cover. He flipped to the poem page and gave it back to Jordanna as he described how the book came to life and wrote before their eyes. Jordanna read the poem and sat silently.

"For now, we will keep this between us."

Ethan and Hayley nodded in agreement.

"It appears you've received a significant gift, Ethan Fox. But until we are sure its intentions are pure, I will keep it for now. You and Hayley will accompany my team to the Silent Forest." She tapped her ELMO device. "Please have Daavic, Nicholas, Gruggins, Azron, and RGB report to the study at once."

THE HELL-GIANT

They rushed into the study, and the others soon joined. The in-door opened, and Ethan's gaze went up as Azron's enormous frame entered.

"I believe you've met Azron," Jordanna said.

"Hi Azron," Ethan and Hayley said.

The giant smiled and winked his single jumbo eye at them.

Jordanna briefed the team and told them she had reason to believe the Silent Forest was in danger.

"Certainly, you're going to tell us more," Daavic said.

"Do not question your mother's authority," Nicholas said, jumping to Jordanna's defense.

"You will book-travel to *Blind Man's Bluff*," Jordanna said. "You will camp cliff side. I've sent for Sol. He will fly you to the clearing in the morning when the winds are favorable. Any questions?"

"What is the Silent Forest?" Hayley asked.

"A hidden ecosystem created after the Great Exodus. The Creators created many secret ecosystems to house non-native species and hide them from the human world."

Everyone appeared surprised as Jordanna spoke openly to Ethan and Hayley.

"I've shown them the portals," Jordanna confessed, "I've told them everything."

The room fell silent.

"Daavic, you will take care of RGB. Keep them balled up until you need them. Unleash them on Nicholas' command. Gruggins, you'll ride along with Hayley. Azron, protect our guests and make sure they return unharmed."

"Mrs. Jordanna?" Linus asked.

"Yes, Linus."

"Do we have to stay balled up? We need to keep our eyes out for Kepler."

"Very well – but remain balled up until you reach the bluff."

Satisfied by her answer, RGB morphed into balls so Daavic could gather them up.

"Let's get on with this," she ordered.

Jordanna held out a portal book, and the cover read:

Blind Man's Bluff

She handed the book to Nicholas and stood back so the team could join hands.

Book-travel was much easier for Ethan the second time, and he woke up with the rest of the team. They were on a flat clearing at the edge of a high cliff that overlooked an ocean of trees. As far as the eye could see, lush greenery stretched into the horizon. Two hours had passed, and dusk was approaching by the time Sol arrived.

"Sol – our old friend is here!" RGB cried out. They had been scanning the horizon ever since their arrival.

Ethan followed Hayley and Gruggins to determine what RGB were looking at. An enormous bird of prey soared above the forest as if tickling his belly with the tips of the trees. Orange rays from the setting sun glistened off his silver feathers as he glided towards them. Ethan's hair blew back as Sol flapped his enormous wings and effortlessly touched down at the edge of the bluff. Sol's wingspan was as long as a school bus, Ethan thought.

"Sol," Linus said.

"We've missed you," Albert said.

"Happy to see you again," Newton said.

RGB hopped onto his back, and Sol turned his head and affectionately nudged them with his giant beak.

"What is he?" Ethan asked as he studied the giant raptor.

"Sol is the last of Earth's mighty thunderbirds," Nicholas said.

Ethan held his hand up towards Sol. The giant raptor bowed his head and studied Ethan. He gently nudged Ethan's hand with his beak.

"Yes," Ethan said and smiled at Sol. "Nice to meet you as well."

"You're communicating with him—" Nicholas said. "Well, well, well – there is more to Ethan Fox than meets the eye."

"Sol, did you bring the supplies?" Nicholas asked.

Sol bowed his head in acknowledgment.

"It appears you've met Ethan Fox," Nicholas said. "This is Hayley."

He bowed his head at Hayley.

Sol was a majestic creature that stood nearly as tall as Azron. Dark edges on his silver feathers made his shiny metallic finish resemble giant fish scales. Black and bronze feathers covered his head in a pattern that resembled the helmet of a warrior. Giant eagle eyes the size of saucers peered back at Ethan and Hayley over his yellow beak that hooked to a sharp point at the end.

Ethan gazed at Sol's enormous talons that reminded him of bent railroad spikes.

"We may be up against a Hell-Giant," Nicholas said. "Which means everybody must do their part." Nicholas looked at Ethan and Hayley.

"We're ready," Hayley said.

"Just tell us what to do," Ethan said.

Nicholas reached into the large saddle attached to Sol and pulled out two metallic objects that resembled giant spoons. He handed one to Ethan and the other to Hayley. Ethan wrapped his hands around the long round handle and gripped it like a lacrosse stick. Hayley followed Ethan's lead and held hers in the same manner.

"We must be in for one heck of a dessert," Ethan quipped.

"What are these?" Hayley asked.

"They are hydrosphere ejectors," Nicholas said. "Azron will demonstrate."

Azron blocked out the sun as he approached Ethan and Hayley. They gazed up as he held out an Azron sized ejector in precisely the same manner as Ethan had.

"Push button here—" Azron explained as he used his thumb to push a red button on the ejector's handle.

Ethan caressed the smooth handle with his fingers and found the button as he kept his eyes on Azron. He mimicked Azron and held down the button with his thumb. A small sphere of water grew in the bowl of Ethan's ejector. The hydrosphere grew to the size of a grapefruit.

"When balled-water stop – launch," Azron sprang forward and catapulted his basketball-sized hydrosphere into the air. The ball of water shot from Azron's ejector and continued to grow as it flew through the air, growing to the size of a truck before hitting the forest below.

"Awesome!" Ethan shouted as he launched a hydrosphere that sailed as if propelled by an invisible rocket and grew to the size of a mammoth boulder.

"Hell-Giant no like balled-water. Har, harr, harrr!" Azron roared.

Ethan and Hayley practiced for another hour, flinging hydrospheres into the forest. The progress they made in such short order pleased Nicholas.

Day turned to night, and the team gathered around a colorful campfire RGB had made. They were in a base camp of some sort, and oval huts resembling giant half-buried eggs circled the fire pit – two of the huts were big enough for Azron and Sol. After a dinner of grilled steaks – Caretaker style – the team retired to their cozy quarters.

They awoke early in the morning when the winds were favorable for the glide to the clearing. Sol would carry the team on his back. He was plenty strong to take them all, but Azron would have to fly separately.

Sol wore a saddle-like contraption with leather seats and straps they could hold when the team sat upon Sol's back. Daavic rode in front while Ethan, Hayley, and Gruggins sat in the back. Nicholas and RGB would fly themselves down.

Sol stepped to the edge of the cliff, bobbed his head, and leaped off. The view was beautiful as the forest slid by beneath them. Strong wind at their backs pushed them along like an invisible conveyor belt. RGB glided alongside at first but then decided to play.

"Weeeeeeeeeeeee," Linus rocketed ahead.

"Woooooo Hooooooo," Newton and Albert followed.

They played tag in the sky and chased one another, doing somersaults and loop-de-loops.

The glide lasted ten minutes before they sighted the clearing – a kidney-shaped meadow that tapered at one end. Sol made a quick descent and set down at its grassy center. The team dismounted as Nicholas and RGB landed nearby, and with a few flaps of his massive wings, Sol was off to fetch

Azron. The return to the bluff would take longer against the strong wind, but the team could waste no time and would enter the Silent Forest immediately.

At one end, a canopy of trees surrounded the meadow and formed a cave-like enclave – the Silent Forest entrance. Daavic led the way with RGB at his side while Ethan, Hayley, and Gruggins were behind them, and Nicholas brought up the rear.

You could hear a pin drop, Ethan thought – but not until someone decided to speak did Ethan understand what total silence really was.

"Mother has sent us on a wild goose chase," Daavic said.

No sound came out, yet Ethan could hear him – it was like dark light. Ethan pondered 'quiet sound' as they continued into the forest. But what it lacked in sound, it made up for in scent, Ethan thought as he breathed in the fresh smell of pine and other forest odors.

"It is a large forest, so we must explore to be sure," Nicholas said.

Thin beams of sunlight peeked through the thick cover of trees and dotted the forest floor. Colorful vegetation marvelously decorated the Silent Forest – much like the Moongarden. Several of the trees had appendages attached to them, and they looked like ears going up both sides of the trees – just like in his dad's sketches.

"*The Ears on the Forest Trees*," Ethan thought.

"They do look like ears," Hayley replied.

"You can hear me?" Ethan thought.

"Yes," Hayley answered.

None of the others were hearing Ethan and Hayley as the Silent Forest enabled them to communicate telepathically.

"I've seen them before in the sketches my dad showed me."

Ethan remained quiet, deep in thought.

No animal life was visible on the forest floor or in the trees above. The only signs of life were the ears on the forest trees and cocoon-like huts that hung high up in the trees. The team ventured deeper into the colorful lush forest.

A burning smell overtook Ethan's senses and suddenly an explosion of sound ruptured the silence. The forest's creatures flooded towards them – sprites, gnomes, jungle elves and forest trolls all joined the stampede.

"Something has breached the canopy!" Nicholas shouted above the noise.

The sound grew deafening as fire rampaged through the forest.

"As we feared – a Hell-Giant!" Nicholas announced.

The Hell-Giant was an enormous fire creature as tall as the forest itself. It resembled a giant firelyte with devilish flamed-horns and piercing black eyes. The monster ripped trees from their roots and tossed them aside in flames. Fire rained on the forest floor as the Hell-Giant stormed through the trees creating a vast clearing of embers in its wake.

"We've got to stop the beast before it has done irreparable harm," Nicholas said.

"Without Sol and Azron, that will be impossible. And without Kepler, the three pyrodevlins will barely be able to contain the beast," Daavic said.

"They will be along shortly, so unleash RGB now," Nicholas said. "If they can pull the beast into the clearing, Sol and Azron will spot us from above – it's our only hope."

"A ridiculous plan, you'll be sending us all to our deaths."

"Give the order!"

Daavic hesitated, but then obeyed, and bent down to give RGB their orders. The pyrodevlins darted into the clearing of embers that smoldered where a dense forest once stood. They raised their forked tails above their heads as brightly colored balls of energy grew between the forks. The baseball-sized sphere's shot out the ends of their tails and trailed streams of energy that remained attached to the pyrodevlins. They hit the Hell-Giant and wrapped around its arms and leg. RGB had lassoed the giant fire monster and were slowly pulling it into the clearing.

"Ethan and Hayley – you stay at the edge of the clearing and drench that beast with hydrospheres. Find a patch of forest that is not burning and use it as cover."

"It appears to be working – but they won't be able to hold the creature for long," Daavic said.

"That is why we are going to help them," Nicholas said.

Nicholas and Daavic ran to RGB and joined hands with them – a pyrodevlin to each of their sides. A bright glow emanated from the five of them as they worked together to tug the Hell-Giant towards the clearing.

It amazed Ethan how powerful the small pyrodevlins were as they wrestled the Hell-Giant. But they were tiring as the giant fire creature flailed back and forth, trying to break free.

Ethan and Hayley stayed at the edge of the clearing as Nicholas had ordered while Gruggins clung to Hayley's shoulder. They took turns launching hydrospheres at the fire beast, only ducking into the forest long enough to charge a new one. But aiming hydrospheres was more challenging than it looked, and none hit their mark.

"This isn't working. We need to be closer," Ethan said. He rushed deeper into the clearing and lurched forward with all his might launching a shot at the creature. The water boulder found the mark and landed splat upside the Hell-Giant's head. The fire monster glared down at Ethan.

"Nice shot!" Hayley cheered as she ran into the clearing near Ethan.

One of the giant's arms broke free as Albert lost his grip and the red energy lasso disappeared. He struggled to conjure up another energy ball as the Hell-Giant swung his free arm violently towards Ethan, and a huge fireball shot from the creature's hand.

"Duck!" Ethan shouted as he ran towards Hayley, dove, and tackled her to the ground. The heat from the fireball warmed Ethan's face as it roared over their heads.

"Are you all right?" Ethan asked Hayley.

"I'll be okay," Hayley jumped to her feet, lunged forward, and launched a hydrosphere of her own. This one hit the Hell-Giant in the torso and staggered it back.

Albert finally conjured up another energy ball and re-lassoed the Hell-Giant's arm just as Sol and Azron arrived. Sol swooped into the clearing, and Azron jumped from his back. The Hell-Giant kicked at a fallen tree with its free foot, and it ignited and blasted into the air like a rocket.

Ethan saw a red flash out of the corner of his eye. The flaming tree was nearly on top of him and Hayley when Azron swatted it away with his hydrosphere ejector. An explosion of water rained down and soaked Ethan and Hayley. Azron tossed aside the mangled ejector handle that survived.

Sol flapped his mighty wings to gain altitude above the Hell-Giant. RGB, Nicholas, and Daavic continued their tug of war battle to pull the monster into the clearing. Sol hovered above the creature flapping his wings harder and harder as he slowly drifted down. Sol's flapping intensified, and so did the wind he generated as thunder and lightning stormed from above. He was creating a storm over the Hell-Giant.

As Ethan viewed the action, he got an idea and held the palms of his hands skyward towards the Hell-Giant – his symbols began to glow. A strong sense of fatigue and agony overtook Ethan as he listened to the Hell-Giant's thoughts.

"He's weakening—" Ethan shouted at RGB. "Lasso his waist and pull him to the ground."

RGB followed Ethan's orders in perfect chorus. Newton stopped his energy stream and let go of the creature's leg so that he could re-lasso the creature's waist. Albert and Linus did the same as soon as Newton's beam was in place.

"Aim at its legs!" Ethan shouted to Hayley as he let loose with a hydrosphere that hit the monster square on its right leg.

RGB, Nicholas, and Daavic moved closer to the Hell-Giant to gain leverage and help them pull the creature towards the ground.

The team worked together in perfect unison, and the monster was hurting. RGB were tiring, too, as the color drained from their bodies and their lassos grew thinner. Sol's storm intensified, and together they were pulling the Hell-Giant to the ground.

Then in a final act of defiance, the monster lunged up and swiped at Sol with both arms. He hit one of Sol's wings and almost knocked him out of the sky, but Sol was too strong and regained control as the Hell-Giant fell to its knees. Rain from Sol's storm and Ethan and Hayley's hydrospheres drenched its flames as the Hell-Giant slowly melted away. When the battle was over, a giant firelyte diamond the size of a pumpkin was all that remained of the Hell-Giant.

Ethan stood at the center of the clearing with Hayley and Azron nearby. He gazed skyward and spotted a single giant feather floating in the air – it would land somewhere deep inside the Silent Forest.

"Thank you, Azron. You saved us," Ethan said.

Azron grinned at Ethan. "Hell-Giant no like Ethan Fox. Har, harr, harrr!"

Ethan turned towards Hayley, and something caught his eye. It was Damien, crouching near a bush holding two giant firelyte capsules the size of baseballs.

"DAMIEN – HE DID THIS!" Ethan shouted at the top of his lungs.

Azron, Nicholas, and Daavic gave chase to the retreating culprit. RGB and Gruggins stayed with Ethan and Hayley as Sol circled overhead. Several minutes later, they returned empty-handed – Damien had escaped.

Nicholas sent RGB to scout the remainder of the forest – just in case. After a quick dart about, they returned to report all was quiet. The team journeyed back into the forest on their way back to The Residence, and Nicholas stopped them at the 'ears' of the forest trees.

"Damien has alerted the forest creatures, they'll be attacking anything that doesn't belong in the forest. He won't be able to surprise them again," Nicholas said.

"Agreed, but speaking of forest creatures, I saw no grumplings in that stampede," Daavic said.

"No grumplings are present," Gruggins said, "they have left the Silent Forest."

Gruggins pointed to a bulky thatch of shrubs and waved his hand in a circular motion. The shrubs transformed into a complex of small box-like structures. "They've abandoned their village."

"Where did that come from?" Ethan asked.

"It was there all along, hidden in plain sight by a grumpling's cloak," Hayley said.

"Can't be too careful, even in the Silent Forest," Gruggins said.

"Where did they go?" Daavic asked.

"I couldn't tell you," Gruggins replied.

DEADWOOD SALOON

Upon their return, Jordanna called an emergency CAGE meeting. Ethan and Hayley were happy for the break and quickly decided it was time to find Dakota Drakelan. But first, Ethan had something else he wanted to check out, so Hayley followed him to the front room.

"Where are you taking me?" she asked.

"Back to the Gallery," Ethan said. "A painting in the exhibit hall caught my eye, and I need to learn more about it."

Ethan and Hayley entered the enormous gallery, and Dorkin Drumbles quickly greeted them. "May I help you?"

"Maybe," Ethan said. "I saw a painting in the viewing hall and was wondering if you could tell me about its significance."

"Of course, Dorkin understands significance of all pieces in the viewing hall."

They strolled down the long hallway and Ethan glanced at each piece as they passed by.

"Right there, that one," Ethan said and pointed.

They stopped in front of the painting, and Ethan read the picture's plaque:

Creator Stravis, Savior of the Hybrid Child.

"Very significant, this one is . . . thwarted by the Seers, Victor Qruefeldt was. Teleported the Hybrid Child they did, teleported to Stravis for looking after. Healed the Hybrid Child, Stravis did, and marked him with his symbol. Marked him right here."

Dorkin pointed to the palm of his hand. Ethan's face turned warm, and his heart began to race.

"Th-Thank you, Dorkin – you've been a great help."

Dorkin flashed a muted grin at Ethan and returned to the Gallery. Ethan held up his hands, stared into his palms, and the symbols began to glow.

"Ethan, do you understand what this means?"

"Yes – I do – I am the Hybrid Child."

"That would explain Victor's obsession with you."

Ethan remained silent for several minutes. He made Hayley promise not to tell anyone – even Jordanna – until he could digest the revelation.

They ventured back to The Hall of Doorways to search for Dakota Drakelan. Finding out where he lived was simple with the ELMO and The Residence map. Dakota lived at a place called Deadwood, the twelfth door on the right. They were near the eleventh doors when they heard voices coming from the darkness ahead.

"Malik, come back here," Caden Stanley ordered.

"Probably caught a whiff of those human brats," Blair Trabblemore said. "My father says the Headmistress has furnished them with quarters. He thinks she is a fool for taking in humans."

Ethan quietly opened the eleventh door on the right and pulled Hayley inside. They didn't have time for another confrontation with the hostile Caretaker teens. They found themselves in a dark entryway to another room, and light peeked through a closed curtain.

"Ethan Fox spotted him with two hell-pods, Mother – Damien is working for Victor Qruefeldt, as I've always said."

Ethan recognized Daavic's voice as they had inadvertently entered the CAGE meeting room.

"Daavic reports the truth," Nicholas affirmed.

"Well then, I've been in denial for far too long," Jordanna said in a solemn tone. "If Damien has sided with Victor Qruefeldt, I will deal with him as a Grimleaver."

The room fell silent.

"We can't overlook the news of the grumplings," Nicholas said.

"What about the grumplings?" Jordanna asked.

"They've abandoned the Silent Forest," Daavic said.

"Why would they risk capture by the leprechauns?" Brianna asked.

"Indeed," Jordanna said. "We are left with more questions than answers."

"How did you know Mother?" Daavic asked. "Who told you the Silent Forest was in danger?"

"Let's just say that my source is beyond reproach."

"You're going to get yourself killed, Mother!"

"Enough, Daavic!" Nicholas said.

The room again fell silent.

"Moving on, Fin has reported a theft at Poseidon. The culprit stole several items from the storage vault. Whoever did this used our presence as a distraction – it occurred during our visit."

"What was sss-stolen?"

"Fin will report back when he learns more – but we all understand the importance of Poseidon's storage vault. It was the only place considered out of Grimleaver reach."

"Victor Qruefeldt become bold," Azron said.

"On top of all that," Jordanna said. "We've lost contact with the Outpost. A team will depart for Kraken Island at first light."

The room fell into a stony silence.

"I've yet to decide who will accompany me," Jordanna said. "I will make arrangements and send word once my decision is final."

"You can't be suggesting – no headmaster has ever joined a mission," Nicholas said.

"I will contact you all when my decision is final," she concluded.

Ethan and Hayley slipped back into The Hall of Doorways undetected.

"Hayley, I think Daavic had something to do with the theft. When I returned to my room after talking with Fin, Daavic was sneaking around, so I followed him. He ducked down the storage vault hallway, and I lost him."

"That does sound suspicious. We should keep a close eye on him."

They entered the twelfth door on the right, and it opened to a small town right out of the Old West. Night was falling as they entered Deadwood. They stood on a dirt path that angled left and widened to the road into town. To the right, a plane with tumbleweeds rolled into the distance where a mountain range spanned the horizon. Directly in front of them was a hill with a narrow dirt path that wound its way up to a dark house at the top.

"That spooky old house is where Dakota Drakelan lives," Ethan said.

A candle burned in a window next to the front door. Ethan's eyes traced their way up the narrow dirt path as they arrived at the base of the hill. He thought a curtain moved in the window. Ethan lunged forward and fell to the hard dirt ground.

"Did you see that, Blair? The clumsy human tripped over his own two feet," Caden Stanley said as he stood over Ethan.

"Leave him alone, you bully," Hayley rushed to Ethan's defense, but one push from Blair sent her crashing to the ground next to Ethan.

"She's just as clumsy as he is," Blair Trabblemore laughed.

Ethan rose to his feet as an odd sense of calm overtook his body, and he took in a deep breath.

"Don't worry, Hayley," Ethan sighed. "Caden was just about to apologize."

Caden swung his fist at Ethan's head but inexplicably fell to the ground.

"Did you see that, Hayley?" Ethan asked. "The clumsy bully fell over his own two feet."

"Sic him, Malik!" Caden ordered as he jumped to his feet.

Malik bared his razor-sharp teeth and growled, but Ethan raised his glowing palm, and the brutehound stopped with a whimper.

"Ethan – isn't that a grindle?" Hayley asked as she pointed at Blair's feet.

A small hairy gorilla-like creature appeared on the ground near Blair's feet. The grindle glared up at Blair with its beady red eyes and bared its sharp teeth.

"Aaaaaaaaaaaa!!!!" Blair screamed as she jumped behind Caden to shield herself from the tiny creature. She tugged at Caden's arms from behind and backed away from Ethan and Hayley.

"This isn't over," Caden said as he and Blair backed away – but they stopped when they backed into Azron. He had been watching from the road into town. Caden and Blair retreated out The Hall of Doorways.

"Troublemakers no like Ethan and Hayley. Har, harr, harrr!" Azron howled as he motioned for Ethan and Hayley to follow him. "Come—"

They followed Azron into town. A row of Old West style buildings lined the dirt road that ended at a red barn at the end of town. The chatter of a boisterous crowd echoed from the building on the left. It had swinging doors, and a sign in front of the building read:

Deadwood Saloon

Azron pushed the swinging saloon doors open with a swipe of his giant hand. The doorway was tall, but he still needed to bend down to avoid bumping his head. The crowd got quiet as everyone turned to view who had entered, then the chatter resumed.

RGB were on a small round table in the middle of an extensive seating area. They jumped up and down and danced around in circles chanting.

"Dragon's breath, dragon's breath . . ."

Ethan and Hayley followed Azron to a table at the end of the L-shaped bar. A single enormous chair and several normal-sized ones surrounded the table, so they took a seat.

"Ethan – how did you do that? How did you dodge Caden's punch and make him fall?"

"I have no idea, everything slowed down, so I stepped aside and gave him a nudge."

Azron studied Ethan and Hayley as they conversed.

"Great move with the copycat," Ethan said. "That grindle nearly scared Blair out of her shoes."

"Blair has always been frightened by grindles."

Azron bent down closer to the table. His face crinkled as matchbook-sized teeth peeked out from behind an ear to ear smile.

"Ethan Fox friend of Seers – Ethan Fox, a friend of Azron," he whispered.

"Friends," Ethan said and returned the smile.

"Azron CAGE member," he said. "Azron brother Gaball become cyclops – twice size Azron."

"I'm sorry," Ethan frowned.

"Terrible what they did to him," Hayley said.

Brianna and Nicholas arrived and were surprised to find Ethan and Hayley with Azron.

"Dragon's breath, everybody?" Brianna asked.

"Do they have sugar-pickle soda?" Hayley asked.

"Sure," Brianna said and smiled at Hayley. "Same for you, dear?" she asked Ethan.

Ethan nodded.

Brianna returned to the table carrying an enormous goblet of dragon's breath for Azron. A bartender followed with two normal-sized goblets.

A thick fog wafted from the goblets of dragon's breath. Ethan stood to peek inside Azron's enormous goblet. A glowing purple liquid bubbled beneath the layer of fog.

The sugar-pickle sodas arrived in the grasp of a small, winged dragon equipped with a basket. The tiny dragon landed on the table next to Ethan and Hayley.

"Two sugar-pickle sodas," the dragon said.

"This is Tinx," Brianna said. "Tinx, meet Ethan and Hayley."

"A pleasure to meet you," Tinx said.

Tinx was a winged pixie-dragon about four inches tall and six inches long. Her lizard-like skin was peach colored with white swirls.

"If you need anything else, just ask," Tinx said as she smiled and then flew off to continue her aerial deliveries.

"To the successful dousing of a Hell-Giant," Nicholas said as he raised his goblet. "You two performed admirably in the face of impending danger," he said to Ethan and Hayley.

They clanked their drinks together and gulped away.

"Ahhhhh – nothing like the clarity that comes from that first sip," Nicholas said.

"What brings the two of you here?" Brianna asked Ethan and Hayley.

"We came with Azron. After we had a run-in with Blair Trabblemore and her bully puppet Caden."

"I will speak with the Trabblemores," Brianna offered. "They've sowed trouble for far too long."

They made small talk for another round, but Ethan sensed what was really on their minds – who was accompanying Jordanna to Kraken Island?

They exited the Deadwood Saloon, and Brianna stepped off the wooden sidewalk and turned to say something but stopped dead in her tracks. Her black tongue lashed out and whipped wildly as she began to speak.

"Ssss-send for help—" Brianna struggled to spit out the words as she pointed at the saloon sign.

"What's wrong?" Ethan asked. "You haven't seen a raven before?"

"Not a raven," Nicholas said. "That is a grimtailed dread, and wherever they are seen—darkness follows."

DARKNESS FOLLOWS

Grimtailed dread was a fitting name for this creature. It was larger than a raven and looked more dead than alive. An opaque white film covered its eyes, like that on a dead fish. Tattered feathers clung to its body like someone had put it through a shredder. The only evidence that this bird was alive was its beating heart visible through a gaping wound in its abdomen.

"Contact Jordanna at once while I fetch RGB. Azron, you and Brianna protect the children at all costs," Nicholas ordered.

Brianna called Jordanna on her ELMO. Azron took up a position next to Ethan and Hayley while Nicholas ran back into the Deadwood Saloon.

"CAW-CAW—" the grimtailed dread shrieked. It bobbed its head and then took flight and sailed past Dakota

Drakelan's house over the planes. The dread disappeared, and a swirling gray vortex appeared in the sky. A strong wind gusted from its black center as the vortex grew larger. It resembled a small hurricane turned sideways in the evening sky. Tumbleweeds blew through town as the gusts grew stronger, and then the wind stopped, leaving only an eerie calm.

"Send a sss-security detail at once."

Nicholas rushed through the swinging doors, and RGB were right behind him, eager for action. They stared up at the swirling vortex, and the stillness in the air was unsettling – like the calm before the storm.

Thunderous noises erupted from the vortex as creatures flooded from its blackness. Vampires swarmed the sky, gliding on enormous bat wings. Vicious flying monkeys carried stones, and giant horned birds dropped off ground troops – armored trolls armed with staffs that spewed blue bolts of electricity. An army of trolls assembled on the planes outside of town – they were preparing to attack.

"RGB, protect the children," Nicholas said.

RGB darted into a triangle formation around Ethan and Hayley.

"Let them bring the fight to us," Nicholas shouted as he stretched out his wings. "Brianna, you and I will concentrate on the air assault. Azron will handle the trolls, and RGB will handle anything that gets by our defenses."

Nicholas flapped his bulky angelic wings and swiftly took to the sky. Brianna and Azron started down the road out of town. Brianna took a position at the edge of town while Azron continued to the planes to greet the approaching trolls.

The flying monkeys dropped enormous stones on Azron from above, but he dodged and swatted the stones with his massive hands as he ran towards the trolls. Nicholas swooped in behind the monkeys and ripped the wings from the ones he could catch. Brianna had an attack of her own as the tube-like worms on her head pointed skyward and glowed. Green pulses of light shot at the monkeys' eyes and blinded them instantly. With each shot, the worms lost their glow, only to regenerate and shoot again. RGB shot fireballs at the monkeys as they continued the onslaught.

"We've got to do something to help," Ethan said. He couldn't sit by idly while the CAGE members risked their lives to protect him.

"I've got an idea," Hayley said. She pulled out her copycat, and it morphed into a hydrosphere ejector.

"Here, you launch farther than I do," Hayley said. She handed it to Ethan, and he lobbed water boulders at the incoming attackers.

Azron arrived at the army of trolls as they leveled their staffs at him and fired. The jolts of blue electricity struck Azron but did little more than anger him. He swung his arms like giant clubs sending trolls flying in all directions. Wave after wave of trolls attacked, but they were no match for Azron.

As the battle raged on, Brianna and Nicholas handled the attacking squadron of flying monkeys, but the bulk of Grimleavers in the sky had not yet attacked. The vampires viewed the battle from above, hovering in a tight formation as if protecting something – a chill crept up Ethan's spine.

"Take this—" Ethan said to Hayley as he handed her the hydrosphere ejector so she could take over the launch duties.

"What's wrong?" Hayley asked.

Ethan did not answer. He raised his palms skyward, and they began to glow as he fell into a trance. Ethan was somewhere else for about a minute before he snapped out of it.

"He's here!" Ethan cried out. "Victor Qruefeldt is here!"

The swarming mass of vampires hovering in the sky broke formation. They were attacking, and they headed straight towards Ethan and Hayley.

"RGB!" Ethan shouted, and the pyrodevlins turned to face Ethan.

"Albert, Linus, Newton – take the attack to them – up there. They will overwhelm Nicholas without you. You must help him." Ethan said and pointed at the approaching vampire swarm. The pyrodevlins understood and took to the sky like three guided missiles.

"Hayley, I have an idea," Ethan said. "Dakota Drakelan – I think he will help. Do you think you can make it up that hill while Brianna and I cover you?"

"No problem," Hayley said as she handed the ejector back to Ethan, and they ran towards Brianna.

RGB were much faster and nimbler than the attacking Grimleavers. They could dart between the vampire swarm and hit them with bursts of energy from their forked tails.

Between RGB and Nicholas, vampires were raining from the sky.

"Brianna—" Ethan shouted as they approached her from behind.

"You two should be with RGB."

"No time for that—" Ethan interrupted. "They're helping Nicholas. Hayley is going to run up that hill and ask for Dakota Drakelan's help while we provide cover."

Brianna peered into the sky. Between RGB and Nicholas, the vampires had their hands full, but there were too many of them. She glanced up the hill and then to Ethan.

"Super idea," Brianna said. "Hurry up that hill, girl."

Brianna and Ethan provided cover as Hayley zig-zagged up the hill. Ethan glanced out to check how Azron was doing, and a battalion of much larger trolls was sneaking up on his flank.

"Azron's in trouble!" Ethan screamed.

"Ogres!" Brianna shouted back. "He doesn't see them. They'll tear him apart!"

Brianna aimed her worm-beams at the advancing ogre army.

"My beams are of no use—" Brianna cried. "I'm too low on energy, and they're too far out."

"I've got an idea," Ethan said as he flipped his hydrosphere ejector upside down.

"Bowling for ogres!" he shouted as he rolled a hydrosphere with all his might.

The ball of water hit the ground and rolled like a bullet car speeding across the plane, gathering dust as it grew into a gigantic ball of mud. Ethan launched three more before the first one went SPLAT. One by one, the giant mudballs hit their mark and left the army of ogres wallowing in an ocean of mud – like a giant litter of pigs.

"Nice bowling," Brianna shouted back to Ethan with a wink.

Ethan stopped and glanced toward Dakota Drakelan's place. Powerful bolts of lightning burst skyward from behind the house.

The vampires turned around as if an unheard voice had called them. They were heading towards the vortex – the Grimleavers were retreating.

The giant horned birds swooped down to pick up the trolls while vampires collected their fallen brothers. The Grimleavers were disappearing into the vortex as the Caretaker security detail arrived. There was not much for them to do but witness the Grimleavers retreat.

Nicholas and RGB landed beside Ethan and Brianna. Hayley ran down the hill to join them. They stood and viewed the retreat as they fought to catch their breath. The thud of giant footsteps filled the air as Azron approached.

"Azron no see ogres," he said as he gazed down at Ethan. "Ethan Fox save Azron. Azron owe Ethan Fox life."

"You owe me nothing."

Azron studied Ethan and blinked his sizable eye as a smile formed on his lips.

"Ogres no like Ethan Fox. Har, harr, harrr!"

Ethan, Hayley, and Brianna all laughed with Azron, but Nicholas was deep in thought.

"My tactics were all wrong. If RGB hadn't joined me in the air, you'd have all perished."

"Ethan Fox saved the day when he sent RGB to help you . . . and Hayley to sss-solicit Dakota Drakelan's help."

"Brilliant decision," Nicholas said to Ethan. "I guess I owe you one as well."

Ethan smiled, then turned to Hayley.

"You found Dakota Drakelan?" he asked.

"Dakota Drakelan?"

"Yes – when you ran up the hill for help," Ethan said.

"I – I don't remember. The last thing I remember is running up the hill."

"Dakota no want be found," Azron said.

"What happened to you?" Hayley asked Ethan. "You fell into a trance."

"The Seers – I had a vision, and vampires overran us, so I told RGB to help Nicholas when they attacked."

Nicholas and Brianna exchanged glances at the mention of the Seers.

"Beyond reproach indeed," Nicholas whispered to Brianna.

"Something else happened – after the vision, I sensed Victor Qruefeldt and could sense his thoughts. He's frightened – terrified of the Caretakers unlocking the portals."

"Sss-surely, Victor understands that it is beyond our control."

The calm silence returned as the last Grimleaver disappeared into the vortex. A strong gust of wind sucked the tumbleweeds in the opposite direction. The vortex was shrinking, and within an instant, it was gone.

"What I'd like to find out is where did that dread come from?" Brianna asked.

Brianna contacted Jordanna to report what had happened.

"I trust you thwarted the attack without much difficulty," Jordanna said.

"More or less," Brianna said. "But how did you know?"

"Because it was not an attack, it was a diversion. Report to the front room at once – and bring the others."

The team rushed to the front room. Jordanna was picking up the pieces of Gruggins' crushed box when they arrived.

"Daavic tried to stop him—" Jordanna said, "a struggle ensued, and Daavic gave chase, but I'm afraid he's escaped to the Moongarden."

"Stop who? What happened here?" Nicholas asked.

"What has happened to Gruggins?" Hayley asked with concern.

"Damien – he's abducted Gruggins," Jordanna answered.

LAIR OF THE SPIDER GECKO

The Grimleavers had used the attack as a distraction so Damien could abduct Gruggins. But why? It didn't make sense, and Hayley took the news especially hard.

"Ethan Fox communicates with Seers," Nicholas said to Jordanna. "No doubt the boy is your secret source that is beyond reproach—"

"This must remain a secret. You will speak of this to no one."

"The boy can also sss-sense Victor Qruefeldt's thoughts."

"I'm not crazy – you have to believe me," Ethan said. "He believes you can open the portals, and that terrifies him."

Jordanna studied Ethan, her eyebrows raised as she pursed her lips.

"But we cannot, and even if it were possible, I cannot think of a reason why we would. Discovering the portal prophecies is the normal order according to the Book of Creators . . ."

Daavic returned to the study. Although he had chased Damien to the Moongarden, his brother had given him the slip.

"I've made my decision," said Jordanna. "Nicholas, Ethan, and Hayley will accompany me while the rest of you find Gruggins. We depart for Kraken Island at first sun."

"But Mother, this is preposterous," Daavic protested. "We should abandon the mission altogether."

"We must learn what has happened to the Outpost," Nicholas said.

"I've made my decision," Jordanna said.

Ethan woke to find his pocket tote had once again been disturbed, but this time the intruder had knocked over the inkwell, and small peanut-sized footprints trailed ink across the dresser. Whoever had snooped in Ethan's room was small.

Jordanna was alone in the study when Ethan and Hayley arrived. She held out the poem book for Ethan. He reached out, and Jordanna grasped his wrist with her free hand. She slowly rolled Ethan's hand over, exposing the small white symbol in his palm. Jordanna released her grip and grinned at Ethan as she handed him the poem book.

"You've been given an extraordinary gift. You are an essential part of what is to come, Ethan Fox."

Nicholas arrived shortly after that. Hayley wanted to stay with the others to find Gruggins, but Ethan convinced her they should stick together. They'd book-travel to *One Two-Tree Island*, a micro-island in the middle of the Pacific. Fin would send a team of seaskippers to take them the rest of the way.

This time Jordanna did the honors. She opened the portal book, and in a flash, they were gone.

Ethan woke to a soft breeze tickling his hair as the sun glistened off his forehead. He was the first to awaken this time. *One Two-Tree Island* was a small patch of sand no bigger than a basketball court. Two palm trees stood at its center and leaned across one another in a perfect figure X – the only thing missing was the message in a bottle.

The others awoke shortly after Ethan. They scanned the horizon for Fin's greeting party, an approaching hydromorph cracked the smooth glassy surface of the water as it breached. A lone porpoise swam towards the small island. Four humps beneath the water's surface followed along like approaching speed bumps. The porpoise surfed to the edge of the beach, morphed mid-swim, and waded the last few feet.

"I'm Wilbert Frye," he said.

Wilbert was yellow and white with orange markings. He was much smaller than the other hydromorphs they had seen. Wilbert Frye was a pygmy hydromorph.

"Four seaskippers as requested," Wilbert said as he pointed at the strange sea creatures.

The seaskippers glided effortlessly below the water's surface. They resembled giant stingrays with longer wings and shorter bodies – like underwater stealth bombers. The seaskippers were navy blue with red circles scattered across their enormous wingspan.

"Ever ridden a seaskipper?" Wilbert asked.

"Never," Ethan said.

"That would make us all," Jordanna said.

"They are easy-peasy to ride – I'll show you," Wilbert said and motioned Ethan to the surf.

Two seaskippers joined them at the water's edge. Wilbert stepped on one's back where two foot-shaped orifices swallowed Wilbert's feet to his shins – like ski boots.

"Gross, the inside is all gooey," Ethan laughed as he slipped his foot in.

"Now, lean back and steer," Wilbert said.

Ethan thought Wilbert was going to fall as he leaned back, but a thick flap of seaskipper skin popped up beneath his rear like a captain's chair. Two long antennas whipped around from the front of the seaskipper. Wilbert caught one in each hand and steered like they were a horse's reins.

Riding seaskippers was relatively easy, as Wilbert had promised. Besides, they didn't need to steer as the seaskippers had already plotted the way to Kraken Island. They glided over the ocean as if skiing behind an invisible boat while the seaskippers skimmed along beneath the water's surface. They quickly lost sight of *One Two-Tree Island* and were alone in the middle of the Pacific.

"How much farther?" Hayley called out. "I don't see any sign of land."

A giant hole formed in the water, wide enough to drive a bus into, so the seaskippers headed right for it.

"I think you spoke too soon," Ethan shouted to Hayley.

"Hang on tight," Jordanna called out.

The seaskippers expertly navigated into the giant swirling funnel and descended at a steep angle. Spiraling down the edges of the tunnel, like they were skiing down the inside of a giant straw. The tunnel leveled out and angled towards the surface. Everything got brighter as they approached the light at the end of the tunnel and neared a dead-end; a brightly lit wall of water.

The seaskippers joined formation one behind the other in a single file. Then one by one, they catapulted their riders at the wall of water and broke formation.

Ethan hit the water like he had jumped from a cliff. He found himself swimming in a small lagoon surrounded on three sides by thick foliage. The fourth side was a small beach that ended at a cliff that circled the island. A dark cave was visible at the base of the cliff.

"The only way to the island's interior is through that cave," Jordanna said.

"We'll need sunlight crystals," Nicholas said.

Nicholas walked to the base of the cliff and hammered at a gigantic boulder. He chipped off pieces, picked through the pile of rubble, and returned with four dirty crystals he washed in the lagoon. They shimmered like diamonds as he laid them out on a handkerchief.

"Sunlight crystals store the sun's rays," he said to Ethan.

Nicholas gathered the sunlight crystals and handed them each one. As they reached the entrance of the cave, Nicholas disappeared inside and emerged with four lantern enclosures. He opened one up and put his sunlight crystal inside. They all did the same.

"Sunlight crystals emit sunlight," he said as they entered the cave.

The crystals fired up and lit the cave like a propane lantern. The cave was straight and narrow but widened as they reached a fork in its path.

"We must take the path to the right," Jordanna said. "A fearsome creature lives within this cave – the path to the left is home to the fabled spider gecko."

They continued to the right, but a cave-in had blocked the path.

"We should fear the worst and prepare for a dangerous journey," Jordanna said.

"Agreed, we'll have to risk the other tunnel. The children will be safe at the lagoon. We will send for them once we've reached the Outpost."

"No – you can't leave us behind at the first sign of danger," Hayley said.

"Besides, you might need us," Ethan said.

"I understand your disappointment, but I won't risk your safety – we will send for you shortly."

Ethan and Hayley were back at the beach, and Nicholas and Jordanna had ventured into the lair. The spider gecko slept most of the time but always woke up hungry, Jordanna had explained.

Nearly an hour had passed, and Ethan and Hayley were impatient.

"Something's not right," Hayley said.

"Your ring again?"

"No, just an intuition that my mother brought us along for a reason."

"I've been thinking the same thing. When Jordanna gave the poem book back to me, she saw my palm symbols and said I was an important part of what was to come."

"They need our help, Ethan. She must have felt strongly about that, or we wouldn't be here."

Ethan and Hayley scooped up their sunlight crystals and retraced their way to the fork, where they ventured into the lair of the spider gecko. They trodded lightly and made as little noise as possible. The cave opened to a chamber the size of a living room. Their lanterns did not light the entire chamber, so Ethan veered left while Hayley explored right.

"Ethan," Hayley whispered.

Ethan peered across the chamber to determine what she had found. A pirate's remains were pinned to the cave wall in a sitting position, held in place by thick webbing. The skeleton wore tattered clothes and clutched a jeweled dagger in his hand.

Ethan hurried to Hayley's side, and a glittering patch of gold materialized on the cave wall; a circular pattern of gold flakes above the remains.

"Somebody must have hidden that there," Ethan said in a muted voice.

"The gold is hiding something," Hayley said.

Ethan scratched at the gold, and it flaked away, uncovering a black crest embedded in the cave wall. He pried at the crest with his fingers, but it was in too deep.

"Use this," Hayley said as she handed Ethan the dagger she had removed from the skeleton's hand.

Ethan pried the crest from the wall and held up the cantaloupe-sized object crafted from black marble-like material. As he moved closer to his lantern, a vague outline of symbols became visible engraved into its surface. One symbol inscribed into each quadrant – and one of them was Ethan's.

"Stravis' symbol, I wonder what the other ones are," Ethan said as he stored the dagger and crest in his pocket tote.

They continued to the end of the chamber, where the cave narrowed. The darkness ahead was stone silent, so they crept along quietly. They arrived at the next chamber, and a pungent musty scent filled the air as they entered. It reminded Ethan of an enormous gymnasium with high ceilings. White oblong sacs clung to the walls like water balloons, and bluish fluorescent light glowed from within each one. Thousands of them lined the walls of the giant chamber.

"They're eggs of some kind," Ethan whispered.

"My ring is crawling again . . ."

They were at the center of the chamber when wisps of yellow light emerged from Ethan's pants. The poem book came to life inside, so he retrieved his pocket tote and drew it open. He held the book out in his empty hands, and the pages flipped to the first blank page where a poem eerily appeared on the glowing page. The poem read:

Creepy Crawlers

Dark and dreary comes the night.
We lose our way in fear and fright.

Loud and crunchy noise prevails.
It all begins with slugs and snails.

Death that's black is all around.
So use your light but make no sound.

For if you run away with fear,
Creepy Crawlers will be near.

Ethan finished reading the poem when a crunchy crawly sound began to reverberate through the cave. Something rustled on the ground around them, so Ethan held his lantern out and bent down to see black bugs covering the chamber floor. Slugs, snails, beetles, scorpions, centipedes, worms, and crickets crawled over themselves. They were much larger than any Ethan had seen before, and they had them surrounded.

"AAAAAAAAAAHHHHHHHHHHHHHHHH!" Hayley let out a piercing scream.

"Shh," Ethan said. "The poem said not to make a sound."

Ethan swung his lantern at the creepy crawlers, and they backed off as he pushed forward, making sweeping motions with his lantern.

Hayley regained her composure and joined Ethan with her lantern.

"STOP!" Nicholas called out from across the chamber.

"Listen carefully – place your lanterns on the ground and stand between them, then do not move a muscle."

Hayley's scream had alerted Nicholas and Jordanna, as they stood on a ledge at the end of the chamber at an entrance to another tunnel.

They obeyed as Nicholas slammed his lantern against the cave wall. The sunlight crystal fell to the ground, so Nicholas scooped it up and spread his wings to take flight. He circled overhead, looking for a sweet spot in the mass of black death below.

"Close your eyes," Nicholas said.

He broke into a dive and smashed the crystal into the black mass. A blinding flash of light enveloped the chamber as the bugs ignited into a blue inferno and vaporized. Nicholas landed beside them.

"You were foolish to come after us," Jordanna said.

She jumped off the ledge then stopped as a sound filled the cavern. Ethan, Hayley, and Nicholas spun around to view what was making the creepy clicking sound. The noise came from another tunnel high up on the chamber wall. An enormous spider gecko emerged from the dark tunnel. The creature resembled a car-sized scorpion with spider legs and gecko feet as it crept down the cave wall.

"Take the children and find a way up that shaft," Nicholas said. "I will hold off the monster with the sunlight crystals."

Ethan and Hayley ran to Jordanna as Nicholas smashed their lanterns and retrieved the two sunlight crystals.

Jordanna led them down a narrow tunnel. They arrived at another small chamber that was dimly lit by the luminescence of spider gecko eggs. A thin ray of light beamed down from a shaft at the end of the chamber. They were at the bottom of a well that led to the surface.

Jordanna scanned the walls looking for a way up. A rope ladder lay at her feet – someone had thrown it in from above. They continued searching but found nothing on the smooth rock walls.

Nicholas entered the chamber.

"I hoped you'd be gone by now. I only stunned the beast," he gasped. "I can't say I like our chances."

"Can't you fly the ladder up the shaft?" Ethan asked.

"My wingspan is far too extensive. I would never make it up that shaft."

"I know what to do," said Hayley.

She pulled a squishy glowing egg from the cave wall. The sac was the size of zucchini and jiggled like Jell-O. She squeezed the end, and slimy green goo squirted out. She squeezed every last drop of goo from the egg sac and slipped it over her arm. It fit like a sock at first but then sucked itself snug against her skin. Her arm began to grow longer as her fingertips morphed into suction cups. Hayley had grown a gecko arm.

The others were speechless as Hayley continued with her other arm and legs. She was halfway up the shaft before they understood what she was up to.

"Follow Hayley," Nicholas said, "The creature will be coming."

He shattered the remaining lantern, and Ethan and Jordanna were outfitting themselves with gecko limbs when they heard the creature return – click-click-click.

The beast emerged from the tunnel and was a blackish-purple with a gecko head with six black spider eyes. Three tails hung over its head like a scorpion, two web spinners, and a long one in the middle for shooting dagger-like spikes at its prey.

Jordanna and Ethan started up the shaft wall.

Nicholas threw the remaining crystal at the creature's feet, and a blinding flash filled the chamber, causing the beast to retreat into the tunnel.

Nicholas squished eggs to outfit himself with gecko limbs. He was on his last limb when the spider gecko crept back into the chamber. He started up the shaft with the creature in hot pursuit.

Ethan and Jordanna emerged from the shaft into a bright and sunny day. If Nicholas could reach the sunlight, the spider gecko would not follow. Hayley found a thick coil of rope to tie around a nearby tree.

Nicholas clumsily made his way up the shaft. The spider gecko closed in as its three tails spit like machine guns.

Streams of web trailed out the spinners while spikes zipped out from the middle tail. A stream of web narrowly missed Nicholas' head, but the next one ensnared his foot in its grasp. He lunged forward and broke free, but one of his gecko legs pulled off. Nicholas was losing his grip.

Hayley finished tying off the rope. Ethan and Jordanna helped her carry the heavy coil to the edge of the shaft. The spider gecko was nearly upon him when they tossed the rope.

"Grab the rope, and we'll pull you up," Jordanna yelled.

The rope was just outside of Nicholas' reach. The spider gecko was bearing down on him when he made one last desperate move. He lunged up in one sweeping motion, and his gecko limbs nearly tore off, but his effort was just enough as he grasped the rope.

The spider gecko lurched forward and spat two spikes from its long middle tail. One struck Nicholas in the meat of his thigh. He was using his last bit of strength as they hauled him up. When he reached the top, Nicholas lost consciousness.

KRAKEN ISLAND

Nicholas had a death grip on the rope when he reached the top. Jordanna removed the barb and revived him with water from a canteen. He appeared weak, but Jordanna explained that vamprils have a healthy metabolism, and it would take time for the poison to do its damage.

"There's nothing more I can do," Jordanna said. "We must get him to the Outpost."

"I'm too weak to fly, but if you fashion a crutch, I will walk," Nicholas said.

They were at the top of a cliff that overlooked the interior of the island.

Ethan and Hayley helped Jordanna search for a branch they could use to build a crutch.

To the right, a narrow path carved its way down the inside of the circular mountain range like the threads of a bolt – that was their way down. The mountain range encircled the island's interior like a giant bowl. A land-locked lake filled the bowl, and a landmass stood at the lake's center – an island within an island. A column of smoke rose from the small island.

"Inner Island," Jordanna said. "We must proceed with caution."

They made their way down the narrow path as Nicholas struggled but managed with the help of the crutch. An hour later, they had reached the bottom as the trail ended on a small rocky beach with a sign in the middle that read:

Private Notice from Inner Island:

To raise the bridge of water, it takes a special stone. A five hopper is required to make it ring the tone. Skip not once to see it through, it takes two skips from me to you.

"A riddle," said Ethan.

"One of Commander Triplin's extra precautions," Jordanna said. "He mentioned extra measures, but he never gave me any details."

"Let's see," Ethan said as he pondered the riddle. "I think it is talking about skipping a rock. I used to skip rocks with my dad – a five hopper is five skips."

Ethan looked for a rock to demonstrate.

"There is a trick to skipping rocks. The flattest ones skip the best."

He picked up a rock shaped like a used bar of soap. He walked to the water's edge and pitched the rock low and parallel to the water. Ethan's rock sank the second it touched the water and didn't skip a notch.

"Bad throw, needs to skim along the top," Ethan said.

Hayley searched for rocks too, and Ethan found a pile of flat slate. He was on his fourth unsuccessful attempt before Hayley found her first rock. She approached the water with a perfectly round rock.

"They have to be flat, that one will never skip," said Ethan.

"The sign says, 'a special stone,'" Hayley said, "haven't you noticed most of the rocks on this beach are flat?"

She launched an underhanded softball pitch at the lake, and the stone bounced off the water's surface like a ping-pong ball off a concrete floor – a three hopper.

"Ouch, I got told," Ethan laughed.

"Give one a try," Hayley handed Ethan a round stone.

He launched the rock straight up into the air, and it landed with a thud and hopped five times before sinking.

A loud gong sounded from Inner Island and rang in their ears like a hearing test. The water bubbled like in a kettle on a campfire. Pillars of water sprouted in the distance, and one after another, they sprang up like pegs in a cribbage board. Two rows of water columns stretched across the lake to Inner Island – piles for the forming water bridge. A river of water rushed across the top and calmed to a smooth glass surface that rested atop the pilings. Fish swam within the structure of the liquid bridge.

"A bridge," Ethan said. He ran onto the bridge, and it easily held his weight.

"Come on," he said as he stopped and splashed into the lake below.

Hayley reread the sign, and a deviant smile grew on her face – Ethan was about to get told again.

"It takes two skips from me to you," she read.

She skipped up the ramp to the platform of water and kept skipping in circles.

"You have to skip, and you can't stop," she said.

"Well done, my dear," Jordanna said.

Nicholas was barely able to walk, let alone skip across the long bridge – but with his wings and crutch together, he was able to lighten his weight and mimic a skipping motion.

As they reached Inner Island, Nicholas collapsed.

"Shnickyrooners and things like that," he murmured.

"What's wrong with him?" Hayley asked.

"He's growing weaker and has become delirious," Jordanna said. "We'll have to help him the rest of the way."

Jordanna draped Nicholas's arm over her shoulder. Ethan took the other.

They were at the edge of a thick jungle where a well-traveled path led into the green wall of growth – they had found the way to the Outpost.

They came upon an extensive clearing with a cluster of tall trees at its center. The abundant branches hid a collection of structures with bamboo stairways and bridges that connected seven tiers of huts. The sight reminded Ethan of a Disney treehouse he had once seen.

They arrived at the towering trees that held the Outpost. A giant bonfire became visible – the source of the smoke that billowed from the island. Piles of vampire bodies lay stacked near the bonfire; and a woman knelt, crying, while a tall man threw another vampire into the flames – they wore black and white Caretaker robes. Jordanna called out to Commander Adam Triplin and his wife Trudy.

"What happened here?" she asked.

"They surprised us and killed my entire staff before we even knew what hit us," Commander Triplin said. "They were Grimleavers – but they could shape-shift."

"Hydromorph blood," Jordanna said. "They've learned of its transmorphic properties and are using it as a weapon."

"They were nervous and kept talking about Victor Qruefeldt's fear that the Caretakers would somehow unlock the portals."

"This isn't the first time I've heard that," Jordanna said.

"They sabotaged our communications – we were helpless – until they came and killed them all."

"Who came? Who are they?" Jordanna asked.

"I-I-I don't know – they were unlike anything I've ever seen."

Nicholas collapsed as Jordanna and Ethan laid him down gently. Jordanna knelt by his side as he was about to lose consciousness.

"Vamprils are near," Nicholas said in a barely audible voice.

"Where are your medical supplies?" asked Jordanna.

"Ethan, the poem book," Hayley said as her ring slithered around her finger.

Ethan retrieved the book like a pro as it sprang to life. Jordanna looked on with keen interest as the pages flipped to the first blank page. Writing crawled up the page then they read the words:

The Plight of the Vamprils

A proud but troubled species, secluded and alone.

Vampril wings take flight; they come to save their own.

Dark disturbing secrets, the story will be told.

Feeding on blood of vampires, so ruthless and so bold.

Devolved of spirit, weak of mind.

Like fallen angels, running blind.

The dangerous path they've chosen could surely be their end.

Two outcomes, one forsaken, be it enemy or friend.

"This can only mean one thing," Jordanna said.

She held her palms to her temples as if in pain. Then she stood, extended her arms, and spoke in an amplified voice.

"He will die without your help. He does not deserve to die."

Her voice echoed through the island. There was no reply, but then sounds thundered from the distant mountains as angelic figures flew towards them – vamprils.

They landed near the bonfire and walked towards Jordanna in a V formation. All seven of them were female.

"Valeska, I wish we were meeting under better circumstances," Jordanna said.

The vamprils wore flowing white robes, and Valeska Vandercort was the tallest of the group – she was their leader.

"Tend to him," Valeska ordered, and the vampril women rushed to Nicholas' side.

"Where are the others?" Jordanna asked.

"A terrible thing happened," Valeska said. "We never considered they could hunt us so easily. The Grimleavers have a nose for vampril blood – only four of our men survived."

"You could have come back," Jordanna said.

"We thought we had found a place of safety here, but they can shape-shift now – we won't be safe anywhere."

"He's in bad shape, but hopefully, we've treated him in time," one of the vampril women said.

The sound of splashing came from a nearby inlet on the other side of the trees. Jordanna and Valeska walked towards the disturbance, and Ethan and Hayley followed.

"We've been taking care of the pups," Valeska said. "Since the attack on the Outpost, we've been feeding them."

They came to a ramp that led into a small cove where two sea creatures frolicked in the water like seal pups. The playful young animals hobbled out of the water to greet the approaching people.

The kraken pups had cute faces with big brown eyes and long lashes. They were dark bluish-purple with the body of a massive seal, but much longer and their tails tapered at the end like an eel. They walked on a row of elongated pectoral fins that were floppy at the ends like immature tentacles.

"Where is the third?" Jordanna asked. "Commander Triplin said they were all accounted for."

"As I was saying, we've taken care of the pups for nearly a week. The commander you spoke to was a Grimleaver. They held Commander Triplin and his wife captive when they arrived and took the pup. Some stayed behind to carry on the charade until . . ." her voice trailed off.

"The Commander spoke of someone killing the vampires. Did you witness who killed them?"

"I know who killed them. When I said only four of our men had survived, that was not entirely true. Romulas and three others killed the vampires and fed on their blood — they've become bloodfiends."

"Why would your husband do such a thing? Romulas is a noble man."

"We were on the run and helpless, so Romulas hatched a plan. They would bait a vampire, overpower it and feed so that they would turn bloodfiend. That would make them strong enough to become the hunters and kill every last Grimleaver."

"Then the bloodfiend theories are correct," Jordanna said, "vampire blood transforms vampril DNA."

"The reality is worse than theorized — they've become monsters," Valeska said. "I worry of what is to come when they run out of Grimleavers to feed on."

Nightfall was approaching, so they decided to stay at the Outpost. The tree huts were mostly unharmed and would provide ample shelter. Nicholas was in good hands with the vampril women, and Jordanna and Valeska helped burn the rest of the vampire remains.

Ethan wondered why the vampires didn't burst into flames under the sun's rays – like in the movies. Jordanna explained that real vampires avoid light because their eyes favor darkness.

In the morning, they would bury the dead and repair communications. Commander Triplin and his wife would remain at the Outpost with Valeska and the vampril women. Jordanna, Ethan, and Hayley would return to The Residence and dispatch a team to retrieve Nicholas and the injured vampril men.

UNEXPECTED GUESTS

When they arrived back at The Residence, Jordanna wasted no time calling a meeting of the Caretaker Council. They would meet in the Map Room in four hours.

Ethan and Hayley were in Ethan's room, discussing the trip to Kraken Island. Ethan retrieved his pocket tote and pulled out the jeweled dagger and mysterious black crest.

"This knife must be worth a fortune," Ethan said as he examined its jeweled handle.

"I'm more interested in the crest," Hayley said. "Somebody hid it there for a reason."

"You're right," Ethan said as he stuffed the dagger back into his pocket tote.

Ethan held up the crest so that they could view it in the light, but it slipped from his hand and fell to the ground, landing with a heavy metallic clang. The crest did not break — whatever it was made from was very strong.

"I wonder if we might learn something in the study," Hayley said.

Ethan agreed. He returned the crest to his pocket tote, and he and Hayley headed to the study. When they entered, RGB were arguing.

"RGB stands for Really Great Blue," Newton said.

"Rat Germ Blue maybe, but not very great," Albert said.

"It means Red Goat Baby," Newton said.

"Or Red Geek Booty," Linus said.

"No — RGB means Ranting Green Brat," Albert shot back.

"You're all wrong," Hayley interrupted, "it means — Really Good Boys — so be Really Good Boys and quit bickering."

"We're sorry," Newton said.

"You are correct," Linus agreed.

"No problemo," Albert added.

Ethan and Hayley adjourned to the bookshelves to search through the reference books. They were looking for anything about knives, weapons, symbols, or emblems. No sooner had they started, then RGB began to bicker again.

"I remember, it means Rotten Grump-face Blue," Albert said.

"Ethan, can I inspect the crest?" Hayley asked.

Ethan retrieved his pocket tote and pulled the black crest out, and the room got quiet. RGB stopped bickering and stood side by side, staring at Ethan with wide eyes.

"How did Ethan Fox come to possess the Creators' crest?" Linus asked.

The pyrodevlins hopped onto the study table, knelt, and held their hands out.

Ethan started towards RGB but tripped and fumbled the crest. It flipped up into the air and hovered for a moment before floating towards RGB. As the crest reached their tiny outstretched hands, RGB each grasped a quadrant, and the symbols began to glow in each of their colors as RGB fell into a trance.

Ethan approached as RGB held the glowing crest above their heads. The symbols glowed bright red, green, and blue, but the fourth remained black. As Ethan reached the table, the black symbol began to glow yellow, and wisps of golden light emerged from Ethan's pocket.

"Something's happening again," Hayley said as she rubbed her infinity ring.

Ethan retrieved the poem book and held it in his open hands. The book took over, but this time it flipped to the torn-out pages. The first torn-out page grew and reconstructed itself as the fourth symbol of the crest glowed a brighter yellow. There was already a poem on this page, and it read:

The Odyssey Begins

The journey's just begun but evil's planned ahead.

Behold a Realm of Darkness where the living become dead.

Its minions lurk in silence among the breeding horde.

Awaiting the arrival of an evil dark Grimlord.

Creator from a chosen world this warning you must fear.

Be careful who you trust as darkness will be near.

But the future runs eternal, and a savior will arrive.

A long lost Hybrid Child, feared dead but still alive.

Creator from a chosen world protect it at all costs.

A Moment in Eternity, will tell you when you're lost.

"What does this mean?" Hayley asked.

"I don't know – but this one is not a new passage and it sounds like Creator Stravis was the intended audience."

"Yeah," Hayley said, "and if the future is now – you are here to save us."

The poem book calmed, and RGB awoke from their collective trance. They set the crest down on the table, and it snapped apart effortlessly and melted away, leaving four black symbols that were now separate.

"The Hybrid Child has arrived," RGB said in unison. "Your journey has begun, Ethan Fox."

"What journey?" Ethan said. "What are you talking about?"

"Red Gas Buffalo, that is what RGB stands for," Newton said.

The bickering resumed as if nothing happened. Ethan gathered up the symbols and poem book and tossed them into his pocket tote.

"What just happened?" Ethan asked Hayley.

"I have no idea," Hayley said as she rubbed her ring finger. "But I'm getting a strange feeling."

RGB's bickering stopped.

"Master Daavic," Newton said.

"He's not happy," Linus said.

"Let's hide," Albert said.

Three colored streaks flashed in front of Ethan's eyes, and RGB were gone.

"We should hide, too," Hayley said.

She pulled at Ethan's arm and led him to the floor behind the couch. Daavic entered the study, slammed the door, and strode over to his desk.

Ethan and Hayley peeked over the couch as Daavic unlocked his desk drawer and stared at the contents. He pulled out a yellow journal and read for several minutes before returning it to the drawer. He retrieved a skeleton key from his robe and tossed that into the drawer too.

Daavic then took out a pen and paper and wrote a long note. He stuffed it into a fat oblong envelope and scanned it with his ELMO. Bright red beams danced up and down its length until it transformed. Long thin, wiry wings sprouted from the ends of the envelope and flew it away – right through the out-door.

Daavic's ELMO sounded an alarm, so he answered.

"We have spotted Damien in the Moongarden," a voice said. "He was seen scaling down the skyclimber."

Daavic locked his desk and stormed out of the study.

"Did you hear that," Ethan said, "they spotted Damien in the Moongarden."

Hayley's interest was somewhere else.

"Ethan, did you see that?"

"Yeah – I wonder what's in that yellow journal that he finds so interesting. And what was with that flying—"

"No, Ethan, I was talking about the key. Daavic used that key to open the door underneath the staircase. He's hiding something in that basement, and my ring is telling me so."

"Are you thinking what I think you're thinking?"

"I have an idea," Hayley said as she reached into her pocket and pulled out her copycat.

"Tabby Cat, Tabby Cat, make me a copy," Hayley said as the copycat vanished from her hand and the skeleton key appeared.

"Let's go find out what's down there," Hayley said.

The key fit like a glove, and a musty odor wafted up from the dark cellar as Hayley pulled the door open. A creaky sound filled the air and sent chills down Ethan's spine. Hayley flipped a switch, and a dim light flickered down the narrow staircase, barely lighting their way. Ethan's heart raced as they reached the bottom of the creaky wooden staircase. They were in a dark, dingy room with workbenches on each wall. The sound of dripping water emanated from blackness at the back of the room, and then a rustling noise filled the air.

"Do you hear that?"

"Yes, I think it is coming from over there," Hayley said as she pointed at a tall domed cylinder covered in black fabric.

"Looks like a birdcage," Ethan said as he approached.

"I've got a bad feeling about this," Hayley said.

Ethan tugged at the fabric, and the cover fell away as blood rushed to his head.

"CAW, CAW, CAW—"

The grimtailed dread's shrieks filled the damp air as Ethan and Hayley backed away slowly.

"It was Daavic," Ethan said. "He opened the vortex and is helping his brother."

"We should warn my mom and the others."

Ethan felt something move around in his pocket. His pocket tote was unraveling itself, so he set it down on a nearby workbench.

"You're growing on me," said a voice from within. "I'm starting to like Ethan Fox, or should I say – Hybrid Child."

A small green head emerged from the pocket tote.

"And a how do you do to you," Gruggins McGhee said with a smile.

FAMILY REUNION

Gruggins! We've been worried," Hayley cried. "How did you get into Ethan's pocket tote?"

"Been there all along," Gruggins said.

Ethan and Hayley gave each other a glance.

"How did you escape?" Ethan asked.

"I didn't escape, Master Damien let me go. I've followed Ethan Fox since the day he arrived."

"The negative door," Hayley said. "You went through the negative door that opened up when we arrived."

"That ring of yours talking again?" Gruggins said. "Followed Ethan Fox around and slipped into the pocket tote after bumble-head Irvin gave it to him."

"Why would Damien let you go?" Hayley asked. "He and Daavic are scheming with Victor Qruefeldt."

"Not all is how it appears to be," Gruggins said.

Ethan was leaning against the workbench. Gruggins rubbed his hands together and put them on Ethan.

"I remember," said Ethan. "You were at the top of the stairs and shot me with a dart."

"A harmless sleeping dart – I'm sorry for that," Gruggins said. "I couldn't let you blow my cover. I didn't want me to find me. Imagine my surprise when I found my dart stuck in your butt."

Gruggins held out a small golden dart with "G.M." monogrammed on the shaft.

"Confused me at first, but then I figured things out. I wasn't sensing a tribe of Nibblewarts outside my box – I was sensing me."

"It all adds up," Hayley said, "Ethan thought someone was snooping in his room – but you were just coming and going from his pocket tote."

"And the gold dust appearing on the cave wall," Ethan said. "That was cloaked leprechaun's gold, I bet."

"You're figuring things out quickly," Gruggins said.

"Why did you hide in my pocket tote?" Ethan asked.

"We needed to make sure you were safe," Gruggins said, "and to find out what you would learn along the way."

"Who is we?" Hayley asked.

"Do you trust me?" Gruggins asked.

"Yes," Hayley replied.

"And you, Ethan Fox?"

"Yes."

"Then there's someone I want you to meet," Gruggins said and hopped onto Hayley's shoulder.

They locked the basement and followed Gruggins' directions to the twelfth door on the right. There was daylight in Deadwood as they strode into town, and the Saloon was nearly empty as the bartender stood at the bar reading *The Residential Daily Star*. Gruggins directed them towards a stranger sitting at a table in a dimly lit corner. Ethan felt a tingle at the back of his neck, and then a voice spoke up in his head.

"Stay calm, Ethan Fox," the soothing voice said. It was the same voice he had heard when the vampires were abducting him.

As they neared the stranger, Ethan saw him clearly as his eyes adjusted to the dark. He wore a brown trench coat, a black wide-brimmed hat, and dark glasses.

"The stranger from the Gallery painting," Hayley said.

They sat at the table. The stranger's head tilted towards his goblet of dragon's breath. Gruggins hopped from Hayley's shoulder.

"Enjoying yourself?" Gruggins asked. "I've spent days holed up in a stuffy pocket tote."

"Moments for me," the stranger said. His voice was soft but gritty and sounded familiar to Ethan.

Gruggins turned to Hayley.

"Your brother is a good man," he said.

"But the grimtailed dread," Hayley replied. "You saw for yourself – Daavic is helping the Grimleavers."

The stranger's head rose slowly, and stringy black hair fell around his face as he removed his hat. He pulled the glasses from his face to expose his eyes – one deep green, the other bluish-grey with a moon-shaped pupil.

"He's talking about your other brother," Damien Ravenwood said.

Hayley's eyes widened, but she stayed seated. Ethan jumped from his seat and started for the door when the voice spoke up again.

"It was I, Ethan Fox," the calm voice said, "Damien Ravenwood saved you from the vampires."

Ethan immediately realized whose voice was in his head – Damien was his guardian angel. He stopped and returned to the table.

"He has misled you," Damien said. "Daavic has done a masterful job of framing me, but he made one grave mistake."

"We witnessed you with two hell-pods," Hayley said. "You tried to burn down the Silent Forest."

"Do you remember Market Square?" Damien asked. "Do you remember those trolls laughing as Daavic spoke with them?"

Ethan and Hayley nodded.

"Forest trolls only laugh when frightened," Damien said. "Daavic gave them three hell-pods – but unfortunately, they ignited one before I was able to stop them."

"He is telling the truth," Gruggins said.

"I'm still not sure of my brother's motivation – but in the end, it was the perfect set-up. There I was, holding two hell-pods as a party of Caretakers looked on. I couldn't exactly explain my way out of that one."

"Why did you abduct Gruggins?" Ethan asked.

"I was running out of options and needed an ally. Someone had to believe me, and only a grumpling can see through such lies and deception. I was fully prepared for Gruggins to fight me tooth and nail – but imagine my surprise when he came along willingly."

"Willingly?" Hayley questioned.

"Yes – once I figured out that the critter outside my box was me. It made sense that I'd soon be jumping timelines."

"We never did trust Daavic," Ethan said.

"He showed you the secret wishing well – didn't he?" Damien asked.

"Yes – he said a drink would heal my lost memories."

"He lied," Damien said. "The water in that well steals memories. Daavic tried to ensure you would never remember. I bet he didn't offer Ethan Fox a drink, did he?"

"How did you know that?" Hayley asked.

"But I did take a drink—" Ethan interrupted. "I shared one with Gruggins."

"That is how you ended up with my sister's memories," Damien said to Gruggins. "You all shared a drink from the same bucket."

"I don't understand," Hayley said.

"The well swapped your memories. When Daavic and I discovered the well, we drank from it – and I ended up with some of his memories, and he with mine."

"That's how you found out Daavic evolved your species into a zebra," Ethan said.

"Yes, but in your case, the swap was three-way, and Gruggins ended up with my sister's memories of Daavic, helping Victor Qruefeldt kill our father."

Hayley didn't appear surprised by Damien's revelation.

"Master Damien," Gruggins said, "there are other developments we need to tell you about."

Ethan and Hayley got themselves a sugar-pickle soda while Gruggins filled Damien in on what he had learned.

"What now?" Hayley asked upon their return.

"We need a plan," Damien said.

Ethan's mind raced through the events of the past few days – he was formulating a plan.

"I've got it – but it may be risky," Ethan said.

"Let's hear it," Damien said.

Jordanna had called for a meeting of the Caretaker Council, and hundreds of Caretakers looked on from the packed lower half of the Map Room. Jordanna, Daavic, and the CAGE team floated above them.

Ethan, Hayley, Damien, and Gruggins had slipped in to observe from the shadows of the mid-section entryway.

"I've called this meeting to fill you in on recent events," said Jordanna. "We will start with the Grimleavers. We've received reports of chatter from various sources. Victor Qruefeldt has become increasingly fearful of us unlocking the portals."

Muffled voices filled the room.

"Open-em up!" shouted a voice from the crowd.

"The Book of Creators clearly states," said Jordanna. "The portals will only unlock upon discovery of the prophecies – we have no key."

"Their fear makes perfect sense. Secluded from the elemental worlds they stand stronger," said Brianna.

"So, the Grimleavers have become more aggressive," Daavic said, "to distract us from accomplishing something we cannot possibly accomplish."

"Yes," Jordanna said. "Unless – there is another way."

"If they fear it, we should unlock the portals," a voice yelled out.

"Find the key!" cried another as others followed along.

"Find the key! Find the key!" the crowd chanted.

"Moving along," Jordanna hushed the crowd. "We've received word from Fin regarding the break-in at Poseidon – the stolen items were from Stravis' bunker."

Muffled discussion filled the room again.

"They are still investigating, but Stravis' journal was among the stolen items."

"Stravis' journal," Ethan whispered. "That has to be the yellow book Daavic has locked away in the study – just as I suspected."

The crowd grew louder.

"The Grimleavers have attacked the Outpost and abducted one of the pups. Fin believes a kraken is on the loose."

"How could they attack the Outpost?" asked a voice in the crowd.

"The vamprils held witness," Nicholas said. "They were hiding on the island and confirmed another of Fin's suspicions. The Grimleavers are using hydromorph blood – it is transmorphic."

Muffled voices erupted again.

"We've lost many vamprils – and some have become bloodfiends," Jordanna said.

The voices grew louder.

"Why release a kraken?" someone in the crowd yelled.

"Grimleavers are not foolish enough to devolve an earthly kraken!" another chimed in.

"Another of those nagging questions," Jordanna said.

"Isn't it obvious?" a voice shouted above the crowd. "They freed a kraken to wreak havoc so you would send a team to Poseidon."

A stranger emerged from the shadows above the crowd – he wore a brown trench coat. Ethan and Hayley were at his side with Gruggins on Hayley's shoulder. Damien took off his hat and glasses, and the room erupted with noise as the crowd recognized the man who killed their beloved leader.

"SECURITY, TO THE MAP ROOM!" Daavic screamed into his ELMO. "ARREST THIS MAN IMMEDIATELY!"

Daavic pointed his red gloved finger at his brother, his face pink with anger. The room grew silent.

"I know what they've been up to, Mother – I know what he's been up to!"

Damien pointed back at his brother.

"SEIZE THAT MAN," Daavic ordered as security entered the room.

"I didn't come alone, we can help you, Mother – but we must speak in private."

The security detail surrounded Damien and the others, and slowly closed in.

"WAIT – I will hear what my son has to say."

"But Mother—"

"Daavic – you are dismissed."

BROTHER DEAREST

Ethan's plan was coming together. They had planted a small snooping device atop the study bookshelves before crashing the Council meeting. Jordanna, Damien, Gruggins, Ethan, and Hayley were in the front room huddled over Ethan's ELMO display, watching as Daavic paced around inside the study.

RGB were arguing over a book in a three-way tug-of-war.

"OUT! LEAVE AT ONCE!" Daavic yelled.

RGB dropped the book and were gone in a flash.

Daavic took a seat at his desk and leaned back deep in thought. He unlocked the drawer and retrieved a yellow book; an old dusty journal with tattered edges. He held it up and studied its cover – and then Daavic vanished.

He reappeared a few feet from Hayley, and the yellow journal in his hands morphed into a small metallic kitty. Daavic threw it to the ground. Hayley's Tabby Cat had returned to her owner.

"Looking for this brother?" Damien said as he held up Stravis' yellow journal.

"I've been giving it a read, fascinating, the writings of Creator Stravis. He tells of his distrust of Zamalador, his friendship with Jasper, and how he saved the Hybrid Child."

"Enough of this nonsense, you must arrest him, Mother."

"I didn't make the connection myself," Jordanna said. "When Ethan Fox told me of his dream – of the blue and yellow taletaddler – I didn't consider that it might be Jasper."

"But you did, dear brother – and you had your Grimleaver buddies release the kraken. You needed it to sow destruction so you could journey to Poseidon to steal the journal. Fin had to request a face-to-face meeting with the secret he kept."

"YOU CAN'T BELIEVE HIM!"

"Victor Qruefeldt's obsession with Creator Stravis is well documented," Jordanna said. "He insists that Stravis is still alive. After Stravis' death, Jasper disappeared. If Victor learned of Jasper's appearance, he might consider it proof of Stravis' survival as well."

"Mother, you can't believe these lies."

"You insisted on the assignment," Jordanna said as the room quieted.

"You also sent trolls to burn down the Silent Forest," Ethan said.

"And don't forget about the grimtailed dread he has hidden in the basement," Hayley added.

"Lies! All lies! I swear to you, Mother! He's the one who abducted Gruggins."

"I didn't abduct Gruggins – he came along willingly. And imagine our surprise dear brother, when Gruggins began having flashbacks – memories that could only be our sister Hayley's."

Daavic's body tensed, and a defeated expression swept over his face.

"You made one grave mistake," Damien said. "You recognized the rift-key on our sister's hand – so you took her to the wishing well to erase her memories. You couldn't chance her remembering what you did to her. But what you didn't know—"

Damien paused, and Jordanna hung on his every word as tears welled in her eyes.

"What you didn't know was that Gruggins and Ethan shared a drink with our sister. Gruggins now holds our sister's memories – memories of you helping Victor Qruefeldt kill our father."

Jordanna glared at Daavic.

"What wishing well?" she asked Damien.

"A secret place in the Moongarden, the well holds extraordinary powers, its water churns memories. Gruggins was in the well and intercepted the bucket, and shared a drink with Ethan. Gruggins received my sister's memories – memories that he views differently than she did. The interesting thing about grumplings, they have many special abilities and can see through a cloak of deception – they perceive the truth."

"What are you saying? What did Gruggins see?"

"He witnessed Victor Qruefeldt kill my father. Victor used hydromorph blood to disguise himself as me – the Grimleavers learned of the hydromorph secret long ago."

Jordanna turned to Gruggins, and he gave a confirming nod.

"How did Victor kill my husband?"

"A Heldrik Vonn Grim puzzle box," Damien said. "There was a struggle, and Ryvias grabbed the puzzle box and dislodged the rift-key."

"Hayley witnessed me killing Ryvias. She ran to his side, and before he died, Ryvias put the rift-key on her finger. Later, she witnessed Daavic and Victor plotting in the Moongarden, and they spotted her."

"HE MADE ME HELP HIM! He said, we would all suffer if I didn't – a fate worse than death!"

"That night, Victor sent Daavic to kill our sister with the puzzle box. Missing its rift-key, the puzzle box did not work as expected and transported Hayley through time and space to Ethan Fox – the Hybrid Child."

Wisps of golden light lashed from Ethan's pocket. He retrieved his pocket tote and then the poem book. Gruggins glanced at the cover and mumbled. Ethan gave Gruggins a questioning glance as he opened the book.

"Read it aloud," Jordanna said.

Ethan's palms glowed as he read the poem:

The Hybrid Child Returns

Behold the Hybrid Child, his journey has begun.

Born of pure intentions beneath the desert sun.

His path is stalked by darkness as evil is abound.

But lightness shines upon him in the friendships he has found.

The next step must be taken, and choices must be made.

To bypass the natural order and guide him from the shade.

The portals shall be opened but only by his hand.

Welcome Hybrid Child, from the Eyes of the Desert Sand.

Daavic removed his red glove exposing a bony gray hand that looked dead. He smirked, and his demeanor abruptly changed.

"We didn't know the rift-key was missing," Daavic admitted. "Or your dear Hayley would be ashes."

"What has happened to you?" Jordanna cried. "You're a monster—"

"Why does Victor fear the portals?" Damien asked.

"The Grimlord fears nothing – he wants the portals open, to expose the Hybrid Child and leave him vulnerable."

"All the chatter we've been hearing," Jordanna said. "That has all been a ruse – to motivate us to unlock the portals."

Daavic let out a sinister laugh.

"Here's an interesting passage," Damien read from Stravis' journal:

". . . my distrust of Zamalador deepens by the day. I fear he may tamper with the natural order. Thus, I've taken countermeasures and created a back-door to unlock the portals. The Seers will make sure that only the Hybrid Child can set things in motion . . ."

"But we were hearing about the Grimleaver chatter long before Daavic stole the journal," Ethan said. "Fin even reported it at the meeting in Poseidon."

"I wasn't sure what it was at the time," Hayley said, "but we witnessed Daavic send a leap-letter in the study. Victor may have learned of all this the moment Ethan and I arrived."

Daavic erupted in a devilish laugh.

"Kudos dear sister – I should have cut out your tongue the moment I recognized that rift-key."

"If Victor wants the portals opened," Jordanna said, "then they must remain locked."

"No—" Ethan interrupted. "I must unlock the portals – the Seers are telling us that."

"He's right," Hayley said as she rubbed the rift-key.

Ethan peered at Gruggins as he perched on Hayley's shoulder, and the phantom bubble floated above his head. Ethan opened up the book of poems and studied the pages.

"I think I've found the key," Ethan announced.

UNLOCKING THE PORTALS

"Funny thing about grumplings, they have many special abilities," Ethan said. "They can even read the secret language of the Creators."

Ethan held the poem book up so Gruggins could view the cover. "Can you read that Gruggins?"

"Of course – can't you? Gruggins replied. He read:

A Moment in Eternity

Ethan read from the book:

Creator from a chosen world protect it at all costs.

A Moment in Eternity, will tell you when you're lost.

Ethan paused to let the words sink in.

"This book – *A Moment in Eternity*, has been telling us when we're lost."

"Of course," Jordanna said. "It warned the Silent Forest was about to burn. And on Kraken Island, it told us the plight of the vamprils, and helped me realize that Nicholas was right – and they were nearby."

"It also warned Ethan and me about the creepy crawlers."

"Stravis was the Creator from a chosen world. In my dream, he gave this book to Jasper, and Jasper gave it to me. I think this book holds the key."

"What are you suggesting?" Jordanna asked.

"The book just told us that we—" Ethan paused. "That I, must bypass the natural order and open the portals. Then there's this:

To find the key things must unfold,

at a grumpling's feet the secret's told.

Ethan walked to the front door and opened it. Bright, colorful beams of light shimmered off the metallic spheres and created a pattern on the floor, a trail of tiny footprints that led down the narrow black carpet. They resembled the ink trail Gruggins had left on Ethan's dresser.

"At a grumpling's feet, the secret's told," he repeated and pointed at the pattern. "Gruggins, would you do the honors?"

Gruggins fluttered off Hayley's shoulder and landed on the carpet at Ethan's feet. He walked the trail of footprints – a perfect match for his feet. The phantom bubble followed

Gruggins as he walked towards the black marble slab at the other end. Damien moved the coffee table that stood in Gruggins' path. As he continued, a golden pedestal appeared where the table had been. Symbols were etched on its surface:

A Moment in Eternity

"The phantom bubble follows Gruggins because it is attracted to gold," Hayley said.

"Yes, and when Gruggins isn't around, it hovers over this pedestal – and if I'm right, this should do the trick."

Ethan placed the poem book on the pedestal, and it began to glow as it melted away, and their shapes morphed together. When the transformation was complete, a knee-high golden pyramid stood in the room's center. A hole bored down through the top of the small monument.

"Where did the book go?" Hayley asked.

"I have no idea," Ethan said.

A golden rod swiftly rose from within the hole and as it grew taller, a small saucer formed at the top. The staff grew to three feet tall before it stopped. The phantom bubble floated towards the staff and came to rest in its saucer, where it solidified into a flawless crystal sphere.

"The footprints," Ethan said.

The colorful trail of light disappeared from the carpet as the light reflecting off the portals changed direction. A laser-like beam blasted from each of the four spheres: one red, one green, one blue, and one yellow. The beams aimed directly at the newly formed crystal and entered at the same spot – but emerged split into their respective colors like a prism. Four small colored symbols projected on Daavic's robe as if the crystal were decoding a signal.

"Step aside," Damien moved Daavic from the beams path.

The beams zipped across the room and projected larger symbols on the four corners of the marble slab. They grew brighter and intensified as they etched into the black slab, and then the beams stopped.

Ethan and Hayley looked at each other as they recognized the symbols etched into the slab, the symbols from the Creators' crest.

"Now what?" Damien said.

"I think we know," Hayley said.

Ethan retrieved the four black symbols and handed them to Damien.

"Where did you find those?" Jordanna asked.

"In the lair of the spider gecko, cloaked in leprechaun's gold," Hayley said. "If Gruggins weren't with us, we would have never seen it."

Damien approached the black slab and placed the symbols into their respective corners – a perfect fit. When the last symbol was in place, the slab sank into the floor like a piece of ice melting on a hot stove. It disappeared and exposed the empty wall.

"The Creators must have put that there to project the lock," said Damien.

They turned their attention to the front door.

"What are you waiting for? Give it a try, Mom," Hayley said to Jordanna.

Jordanna held out her hand, a ball appeared, and she handed it to Hayley. "I want you to be the one."

Hayley threw the ball through the door, and it zipped right back – the portals were still locked.

Ethan caught the ball as it bounced by him. He glanced back at the wall where the slab had stood.

"Hayley, you silly girl, you can't go out through the in-door."

Everyone turned to Ethan. The giant mirror had moved itself to the empty wall the slab had left – it had finally found its place. The mirror reflected the portals on its surface like it was the front door.

Ethan threw the ball through the mirror, and it bounced onto the checkerboard plane and rolled past the portals.

"You did it – you unlocked the portals," Hayley said.

The basement door burst open, and a damp, musty odor overtook the room. Loud shrieks echoed up from the basement.

"CAW, CAW, CAW."

The grimtailed dread's call was unmistakable as a black lifeless form swiftly navigated up the stairwell. "CAW, CAW." The dread circled overhead and then broke into a dive that ended near the giant mirror.

A small vortex appeared and swallowed the dread in its path. But the vortex wasn't there to let something out – it was there to let someone enter. Victor Qruefeldt stepped through the growing vortex with the grimtailed dread perched on his shoulder.

"Bravo, Ethan Fox. I couldn't have done better myself."

Victor clapped his hands in applause.

"You've made a grave mistake coming here," Jordanna said as she stepped in front of Hayley to shield her.

"Young Ethan Fox has done us a great service – or should I say, Hybrid Child," Victor said. He scowled, and his eyes glowed red as he stared through Ethan.

"All has happened as the Grimlord has planned," Daavic said.

"I'm sorry, Daavic – but your secret is out. You're of no use to me any longer."

"But Master, I left Poe in the basement as you ordered, and I've been a faithful servant for all these years."

"Poe, tend to Daavic's demise."

"But I'm loyal!"

"CAW, CAW," the dread screeched.

Daavic begged for his life. "Please, I beg of you, Master!"

"CAW, CAW," the dread leapt from Victor's shoulder, flapped its wings, and circled overhead where the ceiling was missing.

"I CAN STILL BE OF SERVICE MASTER!"

The dread dove at Daavic and whizzed by his face leaving a small black vortex behind. Jordanna started towards Daavic to help, but Damien wrapped his arms around her.

"That is a death vortex – it would kill you," Damien said.

A ray of light shot out from the center of the vortex and scanned the length of Daavic's body. Daavic slowly turned transparent – he was dematerializing.

"IT BURNS – AAAAAAAAAAHHHHHHHHH – IT BURNS!"

Daavic changed shape like a blob in a lava lamp. His head smooshed into an oblong blob as the death vortex reduced Daavic to a swirling mass of screams. The vortex sucked him in like a vacuum cleaner as the dread swooped through the vortex and returned to Victor's shoulder.

The vortex was gone. Daavic was gone – Daavic was dead.

Damien and Jordanna stood emotionless. They had just witnessed the demise of another Ravenwood – another Caretaker dead at the hands of Victor Qruefeldt.

"You'll pay for this," Damien started towards Victor, but Jordanna hugged him tighter.

"Have you ever seen a Heldrik Vonn Grim puzzle box?" Victor asked.

He reached into his robe and pulled out a shiny black cube.

"Heldrik invented a very effective weapon, but it isn't nearly as useful without its rift-key."

Victor peered at Hayley and raised his arm. Hayley's infinity ring unraveled and flew across the room into his waiting hand.

"Makes sense it sent you to Ethan Fox," Victor said to Hayley. "I had the rift-key fashioned from his rib after all."

Victor roared with an evil laughter.

Hayley gasped at the loss of her ring, and Ethan could tell it perturbed her. He glanced at her, and she pursed her lips and smirked – then winked.

"As much as I'd love to stick around, Victor said, "I've got a Hybrid Child to kill, and a human world to pillage."

The top of the puzzle box opened. Victor dropped the rift-key in, and the top sprang shut. He took a step towards Ethan, and Jordanna and Damien stepped in his way.

"I sensed you the moment you arrived from the human world," Victor said to Ethan. "When they interfered in our first meeting, the Seers joined our consciousness. I spent centuries wondering what happened to that connection, and Stravis' journal tells the story."

Ethan looked at Damien and the others, and smiled. Then he looked Victor Qruefeldt in the eyes and stepped towards him.

"You obviously haven't read the words of Creator Stravis," Ethan said with a confident grin. "If you had, you would know that you can't kill me. Stravis spells it out, as clear as day."

Victor raised his arm, and the yellow journal flew from Damien's hands into his. He flipped Stravis' journal open, and the book turned brown with gold letters. A bright light beamed from the book's pages into Victor's face, and he vanished.

IN THE BEGINNING

Jordanna held a lengthy meeting of the Caretaker Council following Daavic's death. Damien and Hayley sat as CAGE members. They made Ethan an honorary member due to his role in opening the portals and vanquishing Victor Qruefeldt, not to mention that he was the Hybrid Child – a beacon of Caretaker hope.

Nicholas, Brianna, and Azron were leery at first but gave Damien a warm reception after learning the truth. The news of Daavic's death saddened them, but learning of his betrayal was even harder for them to hear.

After the meeting, Jordanna called the CAGE team to the study but gave no reason why. Gruggins was a no show, but Ethan and Hayley arrived after the others. Jordanna had news from the elemental worlds and was eager to get started.

"We've received information from the Council of Elders," Jordanna said, "it explains why Victor Qruefeldt was so eager to open up the portals. The lock on the portals served more than one purpose."

"What other purpose does a lock sss-serve?"

"It prevented Grimleavers from entering the human world. The Creators implemented a unique mechanism that utilized a marker they added to Earth's atmosphere – the marker attaches to non-earthly creatures."

"Wouldn't that include us?" Nicholas asked.

"Their mechanism can make the distinction between good and evil. The scheme wasn't perfect as Grimleavers could enter the human world, but only for a short time before dying."

"That explains how I dissuaded the vampires from abducting Ethan Fox so easily," Damien said.

"And why they rarely ventured into the human world," Nicholas added.

"The portals also acted to disrupt Victor's connection to the Hybrid Child," Jordanna said. "The connection remained severed as long as Ethan Fox stayed in the human world."

"But now all those protections are gone," Damien said.

"Yes, and our job just got a lot more difficult," Jordanna said.

"Ethan Fox saved the day with his brilliant plan," Damien said.

"Indeed, and I'm still not sure how you all pulled it off," Jordanna said. "How were you able to disguise a portal book as Stravis' journal?"

"I asked Gruggins to cloak a portal book with a grumpling's cloak," Ethan said. "After that, Damien just had to make the switch at the right time."

"By the way—" Damien interrupted. "Where did you send Victor?"

"*One Two-Tree Island*," Ethan said. The room erupted with laughter. "What's so funny?" he asked.

"Grimleavers all hate the light," Damien said. "But Victor is from Hades, so he has a natural dislike of earth, wind, and water as well – and you sent him to a sunny, breezy desert island in the middle of the ocean." The laughter continued.

"Sorry to break up all the fun, but I do have other disturbing news to share," Jordanna said.

"Tell us, Mother," Damien said.

"The lock on the portals shared a linked duality with the prophecies."

"What on earth is that supposed to mean?" asked Nicholas.

"It means that they shared a two-way cause and effect relationship. The Book of Creators foretold a list of prophecies that, once discovered, would unlock the portals. That, in turn, would set things in motion and the prophecies would come to pass. The list would act as a countdown indicator, so we know when to perform the extraction ritual."

"I hope you're not saying what I think you're saying," Damien said.

"I'm afraid unlocking the portals has set things in motion. The prophecies will come to pass, and with no list, we won't have any idea of when to perform the ritual. We must find the prophecies . . ."

"Well then, we've got our work cut out for us," Damien said.

"Does that mean you've decided to accept?" Jordanna asked.

"Yes, Mother."

"Accept?" Nicholas asked.

"I've asked Damien to take on Daavic's role, and serve as my number one and eventual replacement."

"Congratulations, Master Damien. I'd hoped to learn such news," said Gruggins from the study table. He'd been in the room all along, cloaked and napping right beside them. "You didn't think I'd miss the festivities, did you?"

Gruggins hopped onto Hayley's shoulder. "Woke up when I heard my name," he whispered into her ear.

"Glad you showed up, Gruggins," Brianna greeted. "I have a question for you."

"Well, don't choke on it," Gruggins said.

"Why would the grumplings leave the Silent Forest? Where would they go?"

"That is two questions, and I don't have an answer to either. They were happy in the Silent Forest, and there is only a handful of other places they'd be safe."

"Kraken Island for one, but the vamprils are adamant the grumplings are not present," Jordanna said.

"That reminds me," Ethan said. "Why would the Grimleavers abduct one of those cute little pups? How could one of those wreak havoc?"

"The Creators designed Kraken Island to keep kraken pups in their infant state," Jordanna said. "Kraken pups are cute indeed – but on Earth, they grow into giant sea monsters."

"Shnickyrooners and things like that," Irvin's jabbering quickly took center stage. "Have you ever measured the green strip of bacon lips that normally gets reserved for picture frames? You'll often find loads of toad rubbish taped between the pink envelopes of skunk odor that hangs from the fiberglass chair."

"I'm going to miss your keen insights," Ethan said.

"How does Ethan Fox know?" Irvin asked. "I was told to keep it a secret."

"How did I know what?" Ethan asked.

"That it is time for you to leave," Jordanna said.

"You can't let him leave – he is no longer safe," Hayley said.

"Irvin will miss Ethan Fox."

"As will Gruggins McGhee," Gruggins said. He hopped from Hayley's shoulder to Ethan's and gave him a small hug on his neck. "I enjoyed hanging out in your pocket tote – on-the-go adventurer you are. Irvin called that one right."

"We can't send him back," Hayley argued.

"I'm sorry, dear," Jordanna said. "I promised Ethan we would return him to his parents, and I am sure he is missing them by now."

"But that was before we knew," Hayley said. "Before we learned he is the Hybrid Child."

"Damien will keep a close eye on him," Jordanna said.

"I've already made arrangements," Damien assured Hayley. "I have a full detail that will covertly guard over him. And the Map Room has been put on full Hybrid Child alert. If a Grimleaver comes within a mile of Ethan Fox, we will welcome them with extreme force."

"But I don't want him to leave!"

"Don't worry, Hayley. I'll be fine. I am the Hybrid Child, after all." A tear fell from his eye.

"Will I see any of you again?" Ethan asked Jordanna.

"You are the Hybrid Child, and I am confident the Seers will make sure that we meet again. For now, you mustn't speak of your time here – not even to your parents."

"My parents," Ethan repeated. "How did I end up with them? I still have so many questions about my past."

"I'm sure you do, so here is what I have learned. You were born in the desert, at the site of Stravis' bunker. Alexander and Tiffany Sturgis are your birth parents. When you were a year old, Victor Qruefeldt attacked you, and the Seers intervened. They teleported you to Stravis, who healed and looked after you. You reappeared centuries later with Stravis' symbol etched into your palms, and you hadn't aged a day. Ryvias and I learned of you then, and we decided to move you to the human world. Ryvias and I agreed not to be told of the details. Only those close to you would know your whereabouts. But that was over a century ago, and I have no idea of how you ended up where you are today . . ."

"Who were they?" Ethan asked. "Who took me to the human world?"

"I only know of Alexander Sturgis and Dakota Drakelan," Jordanna answered. "But they spoke of others."

Ethan stood quietly, pondering his mysterious past.

"If you've no further questions," Jordanna said. "Irvin will escort you to the negative door – your parents will never realize you were gone."

Ethan made his way towards the out-door. The Caretakers lined up, so he could say his goodbyes to each of them on his way out. The Caretakers were huggers, even Azron, who sat quietly listening.

"Azron miss Ethan Fox," the giant said as he knelt and gently enveloped Ethan in his hands. Azron picked Ethan up, held him snugly against his chest, and set him back down.

Brianna and Nicholas said their goodbyes as well, followed by Damien and Jordanna.

Hayley was the last in line. She tried to choke back the tears – but as Ethan approached, she lost it. Tears streamed down Ethan's cheeks as he looked into her eyes. They fell into each other's arms and hugged. Neither of them wanted that moment to end, but Ethan understood it had to. "Hmm-hmm hmm . . ." Ethan hummed into her ear. He hummed the tune Hayley hummed to herself their first night at The Residence.

"We will meet again, I promise," he whispered.

"Me too," Hayley whispered back.

"Say goodbye to Mrs. Moongarden," Ethan said.

They broke from their long hug, and Ethan followed Irvin through the out-door. They entered The Hall of Doorways and turned right, towards the negative doors.

"The negative third door on the right," Irvin said as they arrived. Irvin saluted Ethan as he pulled the door open – Irvin wasn't a hugger.

"Shnickyrooners and shnackleboxes," Ethan said.

Irvin gave him a wink as he stepped through the door.

Ethan saw purple and green pin-spots in the darkness. He felt lightheaded, and then he was back on the beach, staggering forward as he tried to overcome his dizziness. He almost lost his balance and bumped into something. Ethan's eyes came into focus just in time to turn around and witness Hayley falling down the staircase on the beach.

"It was me all along – I pushed Hayley down the stairs," he said to himself.

Ethan walked down the beach and pondered the events of the previous week. Would he ever see Hayley and the rest of his new friends again? The Seers would see to it, Jordanna had told him.

The Caretakers had their hands full now. The Grimleavers were sure to make their presence known in the human world – not to mention the adult kraken on the loose. Would the Grimleavers come after him again? Jordanna and Damien were sure they would try. He was the Hybrid Child, after all, and that was sure to put Ethan atop Victor's naughty list.

Ethan now knew what his parents were protecting him from, but many mysteries remained. How did Ethan end up with George and Betsy? And how did his dad come to possess one of the portal books?

Ethan would keep the secret as he had promised. He would not discuss his time at The Residence with anyone, not even his parents.

He ran down the beach to where he had left his parents more than a week ago. George and Betsy had just finished frolicking in the surf and were walking back to the beach blanket. Betsy realized Ethan was gone and scanned the beach. She spotted him and pointed him out to George.

"Go for a walk along the beach, Tiger?" George shouted.

"Yeah, Dad, just a short one," Ethan answered with a smile.

Ethan was back with his parents just as the Seers had shown him, and he had missed them more than they would ever know.

TWO DAYS LATER

TWO DAYS LATER

Two days had gone by since Ethan Fox had left The Residence. In the study, Jordanna and Damien were discussing strategy on finding the portal prophecies and the Grimleaver onslaught they were sure would be coming to the human world. Hayley entered the study wearing a half-black half-white Caretaker robe.

"What makes matters worse is the Heldrik Vonn Grim puzzle box," Damien said. "We've never dealt with such a weapon and know nothing about it—"

"About that," Hayley interrupted, "I forgot to tell you."

She smiled and held out her hand. The infinity ring was on her finger. "Never steal a girl's favorite jewelry."

"But how?" Jordanna asked.

"Your copycat," Damien said. "Very clever, sis. You have no idea how many lives you've saved."

There was a knock on the study door, and Dorkin Drumbles rushed into the room.

"Headmistress Ravenwood, a development there has been. A most unusual painting, completed it has."

Jordanna, Damien, and Hayley accompanied Dorkin to the Gallery's viewing hall. Dorkin wobbled over to the piece and pulled back the cover.

He revealed a painting of a dark alleyway dimly lit by an overhead streetlamp. A pitch-black shadow figure of a young woman stood near a trash bin. Her eyes glowed yellow as she reached her black arms out towards a young boy. The boy was facing the shadow-being and held his glowing palms out towards her.

"The boy is Ethan Fox," Hayley said. "I wonder who the shadow girl is?"

"Good question," Jordanna said.

"Whoever it is, she's making my ring crawl."

Jordanna, Hayley, and Damien stared at the painting in silence.

"Well now, this is a first," Jordanna said, "the Gallery has never predicted the future before."

"What do you mean?" Damien asked.

"Look—" Jordanna pointed at an event poster on the alley wall. "That flyer says – Tonight's Performance. But the date is months away – this has not happened yet."

MEET THE AUTHOR

Author Photo © 2024 Edwin Wolfe

Eric Moeszinger—an acclaimed award-winning author and creative force behind the enchanting world of Ethan Fox Books— is a storyteller whose tales are steeped in the essence of his own life. Writing under the pen name E. L. Seer, the "E" representing Eric and the "L" a nod to his beloved wife Lori. Eric's literary journey began in the serene neighborhood of Sacramento, California, where rustic charm blended seamlessly with the spirit of exploration. From Sacramento roots to engineering, his journey culminates in inspiring stories that resonate and give back.

Explore the expansive multiverse of the Ethan Fox *Original Series* by visiting our website and blog, or by connecting with us across our social media platforms. And join us on a journey that glows with rare magic, unearthly wonders, and true friendships.

https://www.EthanFoxBooks.com, https://www.KidsStagram.com,

www.Facebook.com/EthanFoxBooks, ELSeerAuthor@gmail.com,

www.Twitter.com/@EthanFoxBooks, www.Instagram/@EthanFoxBooks,

www.Goodreads.com/user/show/133515145-e-l-seer